PRAISE FOR 1

"Packed with Indigenous culture and customs and sprinkled with tribal terminology, the narrative is vivid, magnetic, and chilling. The author is herself a Patawomeck descendant, and she's combined scant available written records with tribal oral history to inform her creation of two emotionally powerful, vibrant female protagonists. ... plenty of action, tears, cheers, and historical detail work to keep the pages turning.

A disturbing, absorbing, and valuable addition to the literature of cruelty inflicted upon Indigenous peoples."

—*Kirkus Reviews*

. . .

"Lora Chilton's *1666: A Novel* is an historically accurate, horrific, moving chronicle of the devastation wrought on the indigenous population by white settlers in early America. The author manages to take large dollops of shocking history and fashion them into a narrative that moves like a chilling wind. The story is a tragedy, of course, but in Chilton's sure hands, it transcends the horrors, and the name of this transcendence is Art.

—Corey Mesler, author of *Memphis Movie*, and *The World is Neither Stacked For Nor Against You: Selected Stories*

. . .

"With meticulous research, Lora Chilton's *1666: A Novel*, brings to life the forgotten and tragic story of women who survived a disgraceful chapter in our melting-pot history. Following them from Virginia and the birth of the 'New World,' to Barbados, eventually back to their lost homelands, you cannot help but mourn the lost opportunity early settlers had to collaborate rather than annihilate."

—Molly Caldwell Crosby, author of *The American Plague*, and *The Great Pearl Heist*

"In this debut novel by Lora Chilton, *1666: A Novel*, we are introduced to a history based account of two brave indigenous women of the Patawomeck tribe, who are abducted from their native Virginia home in 1666 and enslaved under the brutal "Master" and "Mistress" of the plantations in Barbados.

A page-turning marvel of a historical novel! Otherwise, the shameful erasure of the Patawomeck would have been maintained."

—DIANA Y. PAUL, author of *Things Unsaid*

• • •

"Focusing on the experiences of three Patawomeck women in the latter half of the seventeenth century, Chilton, in *1666: A Novel*, draws on contemporary scholarship regarding Patawomeck and Virginia Algonquian history, culture, and language to develop her characters and add depth to their stories. It is refreshing to read a story about Virginia Indian women in the seventeenth century that avoids the glamorized, sexualized, and racialized Pocahontas mythology and instead centers on the experiences of those everyday people who may not have been so well-known to colonizers but are the true ancestors of most Virginia Indians.... A fast-paced novel that takes the reader through numerous Atlantic landscapes from the traditional Patawomeck homelands along Potomac Creek, to Barbados, to New York, *1666* illustrates the interconnectedness of the early Modern world and its people.

—Dr. Brad Hatch, Patawomeck Tribal Historian
and Tribal Council Member

• • •

"Beautifully written, *1666: A Novel* tells a story that needs to be told....this is a story of the survival of our best selves over our worst.

—Dr. Barbara U. Prescott, co-author of
My Heart Got Married and I Didn't Know It.

"History is usually written by the conquerors, so it is said to be HIS-story!... *1666: A Novel*, an often raw and gritty work of historical fiction, describes the resilience and tenacity that ultimately is OUR-story! Based on actual Colonial documents from the 1600's, this tragic tale often seems as shocking as a sudden plunge into cold water... but then reverberates with redemption and the LOVE of family and friends that brings warmth to the heart!"

—Buddy "White Cloud" Jett, Patawomeck elder, Former Tribal Council Member and Tribal Judge Emeritus

• • •

"For centuries before English settlers arrived to establish the Jamestown settlement in 1607, Native Americans inhabited the land we now call Virginia. Upon their arrival, Native Americans shared their mastery of the land with the English settlers and ultimately ensured the Colony's survival. However, in 17th century Virginia three cultures collided (Virginia Indian, African, and English). Lora Chilton's novel, *1666: A Novel*, tells the true untold story of the survival of her tribe, the Patawomeck. It is important that stories like this be told from a Native American perspective. The Pocahontas Reframed Film Festival supports elevating the perspectives of Native Americans as part of our shared collective history. This amazing story of survival needs to be shown on the big screen."

Bradby Brown, Pamunkey, Executive Director, Pocahontas Reframed Film Festival

Sibylline Press
Copyright © 2024 by Lora Chilton.
All Rights Reserved.

Published in the United States by Sibylline Press,
an imprint of All Things Book LLC, California.
Sibylline Press is dedicated to publishing the
brilliant work of women authors ages 50 and older.
www.sibyllinepress.com
Distributed to the trade by Publishers Group West.

Paperback ISBN: 9781960573957
eBook ISBN: 9781960573117
Library of Congress Control Number: 2023947605

Book and Cover Design: Alicia Feltman

1666

A Novel

BY LORA CHILTON

Sibylline
Press

AN IMPRINT OF ALL THINGS BOOK

1666

A Novel

BY LORA CHILTON

In memory of my parents
&
For Lyn, Charlie and Amy
&
To the Patawomeck women who inspired this story

Prologue

The Patawomeck tribe of Virginia was referenced in many early written records starting in the 1600's by explorers Captain John Smith, William Strachey and Henry Spelman, among others. These men documented their observations of the daily activities, culture and religious beliefs of the tribe. Also documented were the efforts by the Patawomeck to provide food that insured the survival of the starving English explorers. The written history of Virginia details the decision by the 1666 Governor's Council to declare war on the Patawomeck, calling for "their utter destruction if possible and that their women and children and their goods... shall be taken to be disposed of." By 1669 the Patawomeck tribe had disappeared from all colonial records.

Patawomeck oral tradition told for generations since then preserved the story of survival by the two or three women, and thus the tribe, after being sold into servitude and then miraculously returning to Virginia.

I am a member of the Patawomeck tribe through my father's lineage. I first heard the survival story from Chief Two Eagles Green when he attended and spoke at our family reunion in 2007. I was fascinated by the bravery of the women and began to read every book and article I could find. While the women's names had been lost to time, I increasingly felt their story and that of the tribe needed to be told. This book imagines what their journey might have been based on historical records and oral tradition.

The violence that was committed upon the tribe is difficult to read. However, it is important to understand that violence and racism against Native Americans existed long before more modern events such as the Trail of Tears (1830-1850) and Wounded Knee Massacre (1890). The Indigenous heritage and stories were further erased in Virginia when the legislature passed the Racial Integrity Act of 1924 which mandated that Virginians had to legally identify as "white" or "colored" and stipulated that "Indians" were to identify as "colored." The Racial Integrity Act of 1924 was finally repealed in 1966, but the ugly tentacles of racism had permeated the tribes and much of the culture was already wiped out.

In 2010, the Virginia legislature officially recognized the Patawomeck tribe as a Tribe of Virginia.

—Lora Chilton

Characters

A'KwiMex, full name: **A'KwiMex Onks** (*Ah-Quee-Mex Awnks*) Crazy Fox

Ah'SaWei, full name: **Ah'SaWei WaTaPa'AnTam** (*Ah-Saw-Way Wah-Ta-Paw-Awn-Tam*) Yellow/Golden Fawn/Deer. When enslaved, named: Twentynine and Rebecca

Chief Powhatan: (*Pau-Uh-Tan*) Named after the town and river, may mean "white water" and "place where people trade". He was the King of Powhatan, and the best known of the paramount chiefs of the Powhatan Confederacy in Virginia.

KeSaTo, full name: **KeSaTo NihTe'** (*Keh-Saw-Toe Nee-Tah*) Light Heart

KeSaTo WeSKin: (*Keh-Saw-Toe Wee-Skeen*) Light Eyes, originally named **ToWawhNu'KwiSus** (*Two-Wah New-Que-Suse*) Strong Son

MaMan, full name: **MaManSaKwe'O** (*Ma-Mon-Say-Que-Oh*) Bear

MaNa, full name: **MaNa'AnGwa** (*Maw-Naw-Awn-Gwaw*) Butterfly. When enslaved, named: Twentyeight and Mary

Ninj A'PaTa: full name: **Ninj A'PaTaNuiWak** (*Neenj Aw-Paw-Taw-New-Ee-Wak*) Two Eagles

ToDoNoBo WeSKin: (*Toh-Doh-Noh-Boh Wee-Skeen*) Milk Eye, Chief of the Portobacco tribe

ToWawh Nu'KwiSus (*Two-Wah New-Que-Suse*) Strong son

WaBus, full name: **O'Sai WaBus** (*Oh-Sigh Wah-Boos*) Blue Bunny. When enslaved, named: Eightysix and Anne

WaHanGaNoChe (*Wah-Han-Gaw-No-Chee*) Hungry For Eggs (translation uncertain), Chief of the Patawomecks, 1620-1664

Xo, full name **NePa'WeXo** (*Neh-Paw-Weh-Show*) Shining Moon. When enslaved, named: Eightyfive and Leah

Ah'SaWei

(Golden Fawn)

It is near the end of *CoHatTaYough*; the time of Planting and Growing, in *TseNaCoMoCo*, the land some call Virginia. We have already begun gathering the green beans and squash. The corn is still growing and maturing. We will glean the ears soon, during *NePiNough*, the time of Harvesting. Virginia is hot during the summer, so we get our various jobs done early before the heat of the afternoon. There are still fish to be gathered from the weirs, kindling and logs to be found for the fires, grasses to be collected and woven into mats for sleeping and roofing. Cooking for the tribe is an ongoing task. As we go about our chores, we do not realize that this will be our last season of planting and growing, there will not be another harvest for the PaTow'O'Mek. The fishing weirs will rot and the cooking fires will be extinguished.

In addition to these responsibilities, we now care for KeSaTo, one of our tribal grandmothers. It is clear that she is dying. The women rotate in and out of her family dwelling, assisting her daughter, NePa'WeXo—Shining Moon—with the physical care that includes cleaning and feeding. KeSaTo means Light Heart. It reflects her warm, kind personality and the brightness she radiates. Even in death, she is gentle and loving. She has lived a long and vibrant life and is a respected elder among the PaTow'O'Mek. She has been treated with medicinal herbs for several moons, but to no avail. Her lower belly has continued to enlarge. In the last week, the growth has broken through her skin and is oozing. It looks like some sort of gourd or mushroom, with bloody veins snaking throughout. It smells of death. We have boiled the yellow root plant and poured the resulting liquid on the growth, hoping to keep it clean and to minimize the smell, but it is not working. She has also had female bleeding for some time now. It is not the monthly blood of a healthy, fertile woman; her bleeding has been a constant flow for many days.

As we sit and care for KeSaTo, we sing to her and retell the stories of her life, to provide comfort in this time of transition, reminding her that she is loved and valued by the tribe and her family. Our songs are about her children, her midwifery, her kindness. There had been sadness in her life, as well. One of her sons was kidnapped by unknown *TasSanTasSas*—the Strangers who came from across the ocean, and her second husband died around the same time after being bitten by a poisonous water snake. We mention the missing son just briefly; assuring her we would always be looking for him even after she leaves us. Her eyes are closed but she nods when she hears these words. As we sit with her, we silently remember that as a young woman, a deranged Stranger had raped her. He was one of the Strangers who wore the long robes denoting he was from God, but not our Gods, the Stranger's God. There is no reason to remind her of this event.

Before our eyes, she is shrinking, preparing to return to the Earth, except for the enlarging growth that protrudes from her belly, consuming her. It is late in the evening and as I prepare to return to my dwelling, WaBus, Blue Bunny, her granddaughter, asks me, "Will my grandmother die tonight?"

Before I can gather my thoughts, KeSaTo lifts her head from her deathbed and answers loudly, "*MaTa*—No! Not tonight!"

We laugh together, understanding that she still hears what we are saying, even when she appears to be sleeping. I bend down to embrace this much loved tribal elder and gently touch my forehead to hers. I do the same to her daughter, NePa'WeXo, and give her hand a light squeeze. NePa'WeXo is one of my closest friends. "I'll be back in the morning, Xo, but come get me if you need me during the night," I say as I exit the smoky abode. At this moment, we do not know that KeSaTo will indeed die tonight. She will not pass peacefully; her leaving will be violent and unforgettable for those who witness it.

Outside, the warm night air feels refreshing on my face. It clears the smell of death from my nostrils, and I am grateful for the breeze and also for the good life that KeSaTo has lived, in spite of losing a husband, and not knowing the circumstances of the now-grown son who was kidnapped. Her family and friends surround her as she begins to transition. We embrace the cycle of life. We know there are a finite number of moons to be lived.

My family members are already sleeping when I enter our home. I lie down beside my husband, MaMan, whose name means Bear, and curl into his form, always comforted when in the presence of his strength and companionship. Although he is sleeping, I whisper to him, "*Nih Te Kih Te*'—my heart, your heart" as I close my eyes to sleep.

I am having a terrible dream, dreaming that the Strangers have invaded our hamlet with their thunder sticks and fire, that they are surrounding each house. The horror of the nightmare awakens me and as I reach for my husband, I open my eyes and see that in reality, one of the Strangers is standing over us with his weapon pointed at my dear MaMan's head. Instinctively, I scream and stand, moving toward my mother and MaNa, Butterfly, my young daughter. Everything becomes a blur as the thunder stick explodes and my beloved husband's head is blown apart from the impact.

I realize I am not the only one screaming; the sounds of panic and destruction are surrounding me, both inside and outside our dwelling. The smell of smoke permeates the air and burns my throat.

From the crackling roar, I know our buildings are on fire and that flames are engulfing the whole village. I try to protect and cover MaNa while holding onto my mother as a Stranger roughly pushes us out the door into the still dark early morning. I want to go back inside; I need to help my husband—perhaps he is still alive. Confusion and smoke are everywhere. There is the horrifying sound of the thunder sticks discharging over and over and the terrified wailing of the women and children as they are being corralled together near the main community fire pit.

I think of my friend Xo. How will she manage with her baby, young daughter and dying mother? I know she will need help and decide to run for her home, through the smoke and chaos. I charge right in to see Xo holding her infant son and shielding her daughter as a Stranger points his thunder stick at KeSaTo, demanding that she get up. When she does not, he goes to her and violently pulls off the mat that covers her, exposing her nakedness and the purulent growth that is taking her life.

The Stranger grimaces at the sight and, without a moment's hesitation, puts the barrel of his gun to her temple and pulls the trigger, killing her instantly. Witnessing her mother's merciless killing, Xo collapses, covering her children with her body.

I go berserk and jump on the murderer's back, no longer able to think. I become a wild animal with one purpose, to kill this beast. I am no match for him, and he flings me off. I see the butt of his gun as it smashes into my face and then, the world goes black.

* * *

MY HEAD IS THROBBING AS I OPEN MY EYES and realize from the position of the sun that it is now late morning. I am lying down, trying to remember what has happened. My thoughts are swirling as I retrace the activities of the evening. I had been with Xo as we cared for her mom, KeSaTo. Then I walked to my dwelling, the night was clear, the stars bright. I got to my house and snuggled close to my sleeping husband, whispering to him that I loved him with all my heart and fell asleep. Then what? Did I have a terrible dream?

My mind is spinning when it all comes rushing back—MaMan, KeSaTo, such terror—my chest is filled with a sudden pressure that radiates to my throat and tears pour from my eyes. My mother sits next to me, so close our bodies are touching. She holds MaNa. She realizes I am waking up, remembering what has happened. My mother knows me so well, she knows how passionate I am, but this is not the time to draw attention, so she places her hand over my mouth to stifle my screams. The guttural moan that escapes me barely sounds human. As I struggle to sit up, the pain in my head makes me retch.

"What happened?" I ask my mother.

"The Governor's Council decided to attack us since we would not accept their chief and we would not sell our land," she replies stoically, without moving her lips.

My chest and throat fill again with longing and grief when I whisper my beloved's name, "MaMan." My eyes flood, as do my mother's, she saw my husband's murder, too. My husband, my partner, MaNa's father. The image of the gun exploding into his head will not leave me. I reach for MaNa's hand, realizing she also witnessed her father's brutal death at the hand of a Stranger. Maybe her eyes were closed so the awful scene will not haunt her. She is so young; will she remember how he loved her? I hope her eyes were closed so the scene will not haunt her forever. My mind is jumbled with so many thoughts when I hear my mother speak.

"All the men are gone," she says.

"Gone? Where?"

"Dead, killed by the Strangers."

As these words fill my ears, I fall into my mother's arms, my heart pounding as I also think of my brother, A'KwiMex Onks. I whisper his name "A'KwiMex?" My mother shakes her head; tears now fall from her eyes. At this realization, my heart seems to stop beating and I cannot catch my breath. My brother is gone, too? I have never imagined life without him. How can there be life without him?

These words are too much to fathom. How can all the men be dead?

I look around and see only women and children, in various states of distress, crying or staring into space. I cling to MaNa's hand; I will not let her go. There are many Strangers riding on what they call horses, what we have always called *ManGoi TeMos*, Big Dogs. The men hold their thunder sticks as they ride, intimidating us into compliance. There are more of them walking among us. They look at us with menace, are they planning more destruction?

Someone says that our dogs were poisoned before the raid, silencing their barking, which would have alerted us to the presence of the Strangers. Their carcasses are now heaped up beyond the main fire pit. The flies smell death and have already appeared, alighting and buzzing around our dead dogs. After poisoning our dogs and killing our men, the Strangers raided our homes and now they have dumped a collection of moccasins, tanned hide tunics and woven grass mats into a pile. There is another mountain of fur pelts.

Through their rudimentary gesturing and threatening with their weapons, we understand we need to find our shoes, tunics and mats. They tell us we are preparing to leave. There appear to be at least ninety women and children gathered together. I look for Xo, finding her with my eyes, and I see her blank expression. She is in shock. She is taller than most of our women, statuesque and brave. Seeing her like this shakes me. Her daughter, precious O'Sai WaBus, Blue Bunny, named for the blue line that rims her brown eyes, is tenderly holding her baby brother. She is still a child, having lived ten winter moons. I motion to WaBus to move closer to us. She takes her mother by the hand and leads her our way. WaBus has collected her family's belongings and the baby's cradleboard.

Over the next few days, we march south to a destination unknown to us. There is very little talking as we process; as a people, we take pride in bearing our burdens impassively. We will not show the Strangers any emotion or act in any way dishonorable, as these cowards who snuck into our hamlet under the cover of darkness with their weapons of death have murdered our men. There are rumors that we are going to board a flying boat and cross the ocean. But why?

Xo struggles to keep up, she cannot eat the gruel the Strangers provide. In her grief, she is unable to forget the moment her mother was killed and her stomach revolts. It is hard to see her like this; she is in a daze, the loss of her husband so few moons ago, and now her mother gone, too. WaBus straps the cradleboard to her own young back and carries her baby brother to lessen the burden on her mother.

The Strangers prod us with their weapons, urging us to keep moving. They ride on their Big Dogs, towering above us as we walk. They take turns circling back, making sure none of us are trying to escape into the woods. Of course, we are looking for opportunities to escape, to run for our lives. I think about it myself and consider how to sneak away with my mother and MaNa. I consider Xo, WaBus and the baby, too, I will not leave them behind.

When we are allowed to step into the woods for toileting, I gather any small edible plants I see, mostly to feed Xo, to keep her alive. I also gather the waxy leaves of the rhododendron, which help somewhat with the headache I still have from being knocked unconscious. They have a cooling effect when placed on my forehead.

On the third day, Colonel Guilford, one of the colonial chiefs, and two of his companions join us, relieving another man of duty and he rides off. Colonel Guilford is known to us; we do not trust him because he has lied about his intentions many times before today. While we have never trusted him, I never thought he was capable of this evil, that he would destroy our tribe to satisfy his insatiable desire for land. We call him Colonel *GwaKa*, Colonel Porcupine. He has tried to get our land for many moons. He thinks he can own the land, take the land, move our tribe off the lands along the river where we have lived for generations.

There is constant conversation between Colonel Porcupine and the other men who are escorting us. As they talk, they watch us, and their eyes keep landing on Xo's baby boy, as he is being carried by WaBus, his sister. Are the men curious because his eyes are light-colored, or is there another reason? Colonel Porcupine knows us, he has visited our hamlet in the past and tried to trick our leaders. We believe he killed Xo's husband when she was early with child. Why are he and the others looking at her baby now? I feel unsettled and hold my MaNa's hand a little tighter and move her to a position of protection between my mother and myself. MaNa is just three winter moons old.

Something is wrong. I can feel it.

At the next allotted time for rest, the Strangers get off their Big Dogs and begin to walk around the women and children. One of them approaches WaBus, smiling and admiring the baby. She backs away, her intuition warning her, but he reaches for the baby and takes him from her, cradleboard and all. I am so focused on this and trying to understand what is happening that I do not immediately notice that all the babes in arms are now held by Strangers and are being taken away.

There is the sudden, collective realization that four of our tribal babies are being stolen and the mothers erupt in anguished protest, running toward the Strangers to retrieve their children. Colonel Guilford, the cowardly Porcupine standing on the periphery, raises his long gun and shoots in the air, scaring the Big Dogs and momentarily stopping the women. But the thunder stick explosion only delays the inevitable; no one present will allow this to happen, and a melee ensues.

The women charge toward the Strangers, clawing at their dangling legs as they sit atop their Big Dogs. A gang of five PaTow'O'Mek, women and boys pulls a Stranger from his horse. He is being pummeled as they grab the child from his hands. The mother runs toward the woods with her baby clasped tightly to her chest. Another explosion rings out and the mother falls, dropping to her knees before falling on her baby. Her blood flows into a puddle around her torso. I can hear her baby crying, the cries muffled by her body.

I am amazed to see Xo shake off her stupor and leap onto the horse of the Stranger who has stolen her son. This is the Xo I know, brave beyond description. She pulls the man and her baby to the ground. They are wrestling in the dirt; she is strong for a woman but the Stranger maintains his grip until she bites him on the forearm. She knows that if she uses her teeth as a weapon, she cannot let go, that biting just enrages an opponent, so she hangs on until his flesh breaks and he drops his hold on her son. She grabs her baby, who was protected from the fight by his cradleboard and runs in my direction. WaBus follows at her heels.

I am at the edge of the crowd, watching and holding onto MaNa with all my strength, my mother also standing guard. The Strangers will have to kill me before they take my daughter. This is our chance to escape, the six of us together. We do not need words, as Xo with her baby and WaBus run our way, I take hold of both my mother's and my daughter's hands and we head in the direction of the forest, legs burning, but we do not care.

The will of the mothers and grandmothers to retrieve the babies cannot overcome the power of the weapons as Colonel Porcupine shoots into the air multiple times and is joined by volleys from the other guards. The bullets whiz by and their Big Dogs catch us. The Strangers push us to the ground and roughly pull Xo's baby from her arms. We are helpless as we watch the Big Dogs gallop off, the Strangers now in possession of our four youngest babies.

Colonel Guilford looks flustered, his hair askew and his beady eyes darting over us, the captives, trying to anticipate our next moves. His Big Dog is jittery, rearing up on its hind legs, whinnying. Colonel Porcupine is having trouble controlling the animal while trying to maintain his control over us.

He shouts his duplicitous words: "The infants will be returned when order is restored."

He changes the lie. "The babies will be returned to their mothers once we arrive at our final destination."

He tries to placate us, now by saying, "The children will be well cared for and returned soon."

He speaks in English with bits of PaTow'O'Mek and Algonquin thrown in. It takes all of us to figure out what he is saying. He is a known liar, a man who does not keep his word. He yells to his companions, feigning authority over them. If not for their thunder sticks, we women could kill them easily. At their core, they are dishonest cowards. They seem surprised that we fought their efforts to steal our young. Do they understand their only advantage is their weapons? Four babies are gone. One of the mothers is dead.

The forced pilgrimage lasts ten days. The stealing of the babies, the death of a mother and the constant threat of more violence force us to regroup as we march. We do not want anyone else to die. So we are cautious as we walk, murmuring about ways to escape when we take our toileting breaks, taking longer than is necessary to discuss the options. We forage for edible plants while on the breaks, quickly eating any wild strawberries or blackberries we gather. The Strangers harvested the barely ripe corn from our fields after burning our village. Now they act magnanimous as they hand us an ear in the morning and another in the evening, supplementing the gruel, as our only sustenance.

We are united in our hatred of these Strangers. Sometimes I marvel that we tried to live with them in peace, that we shared our food and other provisions when they were destined to die without our help. We value life. We are a peaceful people. Our generosity has been abused, our men have paid the price with their lives, and we are being forced from our tribal land.

We arrive at a place called Point Comfort, having lost no one else to death or theft. We have not been allowed to bathe and we are filthy, unfamiliar with the feel of dirty skin and the smell of oily hair coming from our bodies. I wonder how the Strangers can stand to live without bathing as they do. Being unclean does not seem to bother them, and yet they scratch their bodies and heads. Bathing would help, but they do not understand.

Point Comfort is located on the Powhatan River, and, like our Potomac River, it opens into the Chesapeake Bay and then to the ocean. The Strangers have built a few houses here, and there is a palisade made of tall, thick timbers between the water and the dwellings. Everything is so different. It smells of unrest and dissatisfaction. These dwellings are square, made of timber with clear covered openings. Where our homes are made of bent saplings and woven mats, with openings in the ceiling for the smoke, the Strangers have brick chimneys for their internal fires. We see only men, unclean and milling about, carrying loads to and from the waters edge. It is barren, they have cut down all the trees; there is no escape from the sun.

We can see several large flying boats anchored in the bay, but what we call the wings are not in place. We learn that the white sails, the wings, are lifted when the boats are ready to start their voyage. There have been stories about sea monsters in the big water beyond the bay. Tales of boats and men being swallowed alive, waves as tall as ten men. We have never desired to go beyond our river and the other bodies of water in *TseNaCoMoCo*.

Each of us ponders the future, what is beyond this big water? Our Gods have provided all we need with the bounty from the river and the yield of the planted land. The Strangers came from this big water, and they have wreaked havoc on our tribe and the other tribes in *TseNaCoMoCo*, Virginia. It would seem the place beyond the big water where they come from cannot be good, cannot be life affirming, because these Strangers do not honor life in the way they kill and steal.

I am unsettled about what is coming next. Something terrible is brewing, the feeling is so strong, I can almost hold it in my hand. Can there be anything worse than what has already happened, I wonder? My husband and brother dead; my best friend's baby has been stolen. I am far from the land I know and love.

Does the big water hold more horror? How can it possibly be worse? A chill runs through my body and I involuntarily shudder, considering all I do not know.

Ah'SaWei
(Golden Fawn)

I am startled to wakefulness by the harrowing keening that comes from Xo's dwelling. It has been like this every night since her husband was killed three months ago. It was in *NePiNough*, the time of Harvesting. Now it is the Time for Gathering Nuts and Hunting Deer. Some nights I leave my husband and our warm bed and go to her, silently walking in the moonlight, letting myself into her house. I usually find her on the floor by the fire, covered in ashes that have mixed with her tears and snot, turning her face into an unrecognizable mask of sadness and devastation. Wherever I find her, I only know to lie down beside her, holding her and smoothing what is left of her hair, waiting for the sobbing to cease. KeSaTo, her mother, and WaBus, her daughter, try to comfort her, too; it's not just up to me.

On other occasions in the middle of the night, I have found Xo crumpled on the ground in front of the door to the temple. Inside, her husband's body lies on a suspended pallet, lifeless and decomposing in the company of other important tribal members who have died in the past year or so. After he is reduced to bones, we will wrap his remains in a tanned deerskin and bind it. Then, in a ceremony that happens once every two to three years, his and all the other bound bones will be buried together. When I find her here, covered in dirt and leaves and bug bites, I pull her to standing, take her by the hand and lead her to the creek. I rinse her off as if she were a baby. Her breasts are swollen and her belly beginning to round; she is with child, becoming pregnant just two moons before her husband, Ninj A'PaTa, Two Eagles, was murdered.

Ninj A'PaTa was the acting chief of our tribe, the PaTow'O'Mek, when he died. He was the younger brother of Chief WaHanGaNoChe, whose name means Hungry For Eggs, who had not yet returned from his trial in Jamestown. Ninj A'PaTa was what we called a lesser chief but he stepped into the leadership role for the tribe when his brother was gone. The Strangers were constantly appearing with demands, and someone had to be in charge. When the other tribes in Virginia needed assistance with something, someone with authority had to make the decisions. Additionally, there were the petty squabbles within the tribe that needed mediating.

Ninj A'PaTa, Two Eagles, is the name he received at his *HusKaNaw*, the rite of passage to manhood, when two eagles flew very low, almost clipping his head as he emerged from the ritual. It was as if even the eagles, the most regal and sacred of our birds, were anointing and honoring him as he became a man.

Colonel Guilford, one of the Stranger's chiefs, visits our tribe frequently. We pretend we cannot pronounce *Guilford* and we call him Colonel *GaKwa* instead, laughing at him to his face. He is Colonel Porcupine to us, his wayward hair sticking out in every direction. It is also a jab at his sharp ways, his unbelievable oblivion to our way of life and his obnoxious intrusion into it. He lives near our village and has been bothering us, trying to trick us into selling our land for several years. At first, he brought glass beads to trade for corn and fish. We traded because we knew they were hungry; we didn't necessarily need the beads but they were pretty and we could sew them onto our hide robes along with our traditional shell beads. He pretended to be friendly, gifting the tribe with copper pots for cooking and not asking for anything in return.

Ultimately, he brought papers that we could not understand and wanted our Chief to make a mark on them, which would indicate agreement. None of our chiefs ever marked the papers. We know he wants the good planting land adjacent to the river and total access to the water. He thinks we are too stupid to know what he is trying to do. He does not understand that no one owns this land; this is for all people to share. He does not understand that he cannot own this land, but he keeps trying.

For many moons, Colonel Porcupine came to visit, accompanied by three other Virginia chiefs. They tell us there are new laws and we are now obligated to sell them any land they desire and that they will appoint us a new tribal chief. Colonel Porcupine, with his rodent-like face, has the audacity to tell us that Chief WaHanGaNoChe has apparently deserted the tribe and now the Strangers will decide who will replace him.

This obscene proclamation comes after we have fed him and his lesser chiefs a feast of fish and clam stew, cornmeal cakes and bowls of freshly hulled walnuts. We danced in their honor and smoked with them in peace.

Chief Ninj A'PaTa listens carefully, understanding the malicious intent that is unspoken while hearing the brazenly voiced words and their obvious purpose.

"*MaTa!* Absolutely not, no!" says Chief Ninj A'PaTa. "We will not sell our land; we are not obligated to obey the laws of your Governor's Council." He says this with firm authority, but he is not unduly emotional. He is actually very matter of fact as he speaks, which is disconcerting to the Strangers, who use emotion as an excuse to fight and kill.

"The Governor's Council," Ninj A'PaTa begins, then stops and practically sneers, "has no authority to decide who will be the Chief of the PaTow'O'Mek. I am the Chief until the return of my brother WaHanGaNoChe; nothing can change that. It has been determined by our ancestors."

With that, the conversation is over, a stalemate. There is nothing more to say, Chief Ninj A'PaTa having stopped Colonel Porcupine in his tracks. This embarrasses Colonel Porcupine in front of the tribe and the other members of the Governor's Council who have accompanied him. He has no choice but to fume internally and retreat.

Two moons later, Chief Ninj A'PaTa was ambushed and tortured by Colonel Porcupine and some of his hired hands. Colonel Porcupine demanded that he relinquish the title of Chief, but he would not do so. Chief Ninj A'PaTa was then impaled through his stomach while still alive. In spite of the tremendous pain and suffering, his bowels spilling onto the ground, not a sound escaped from his mouth. He bore the torture stoically as befitting a brave warrior. He was then scalped while still breathing but refused to cede power or acknowledge suffering.

This infuriated and demoralized Colonel Porcupine, who then in anger used Ninj A'PaTa's own hatchet and in one fell stroke, split open his skull, immediately ending his life. Chief Ninj A'PaTa's dead impaled body was left, brains and entrails on the forest floor, to be discovered by women and children foraging for nuts and berries. He died a hero; he died knowing his wife was with child and that he would not see his descendant in this world. His body was collected and prepared for interment, placed in the temple to decay, along with his fur mantle and jewelry.

Although she is with child and therefore does not have her regular moon bleeding, we, the women of the tribe, bring Xo into the *Mesk YiHaKan*, the Blood House, with us. We are afraid her grief will consume and kill her along with the unborn child she carries. It is not without precedent; pregnant women will often slip into the blood house for a few hours of fellowship and respite along with the bleeding, fertile women.

Our time of isolation in the Blood House is a time of rest and togetherness. We have our own cooking fire, and we eat our meals away from the rest of the tribe. We gossip and give each other tattoos.

We sew with beads, embellishing tanned hides for ourselves or our family members and even some for trading with the Strangers. Some women are talented at the precision needed to drill holes in the shells and sand them into little discs and beads; some prefer the sewing that we do with rolled and stretched tendons from deer. Nothing from the deer goes to waste.

Among us, there are artists who are gifted at tattoos as well. Ideas are discussed for drawings of snakes, flowers, or animals of any kind. I enjoy planning and then etching the designs onto the backs, arms, and legs of the women in the tribe.

Girls dream about their first blood and look forward to their time in the *Mesk YiHaKan*. A girl will get a tattoo to mark the occasion of her first blood. On my first time in the Blood House, I had a snake tattooed across my back from one hip to the opposite shoulder. I remember Xo sitting in front of me, distracting me from the little pricks of the sharp claw, used to create the drawing by puncturing my skin as the dye was rubbed into the wound. It really did not hurt at all.

I remember the days in the Blood House with fondness. As the moons have come and gone, I have had feathers of different birds added on each side of the snake. There are eagle feathers, representing strength and a connection with the spirit world. There are turkey feather tattoos on each side of the snake, symbolizing fertility and abundance, gratitude. Even though I cannot see them, I know they are there and it brings me happiness. Xo has flowers etched across her back and down one arm. Over the years, I have decorated many of the bodies of women in our tribe, including the flowers on my friend, Xo.

Our time together in the *Mesk YiHaKan* is also a time of celebration of our womanhood. We keep a few medicinal herbs, barks and leaves in the Blood House; treatments specifically for women to minimize cramps, increase fertility or milk production. Our ancestors taught us that reproduction was not effective during the bleeding time and that because our female parts are more open when shedding blood, it was unsafe to couple. This is the only time we do not mate.

We isolate ourselves for the first four days of bleeding, but with variations in moon times, there may be women rotating through the blood house for up to ten days. Our cycles are not completely synced and yet we bleed within days of one another. We bring our own mats and sit upon them; no need for our loincloths, we are naked in the Blood House. Our bleeding is absorbed into the mats. Occasionally, we do wear our loincloths with a wad of moss in place to soak up the blood, but only if we have to leave the hut to gather wood or food.

We keep the fire stoked while we enjoy this time together. The Blood House is a slightly smaller dwelling on the outskirts of our village but still within the protection of the palisade. The construction of the Blood House is the same as the individual homes, the meetinghouse and the temple. Saplings are cut and then secured in the ground, outlining the circumference of the space. The saplings are then bent toward each other in an arc, lashed together with reeds and twine. Woven marsh grass mats are then overlaid to create an impermeable covering for the house. There is the usual door flap for entering and an opening at the top, allowing the smoke from the fire to escape. There are no raised pallets in the Blood House; we sleep on mats on the ground.

We all mourn the brutal death of Ninj A'PaTa and we give Xo space and time to grieve. We bring her broth and sit with her while she drinks it. We groom her, untangle her growing hair, with combs made from bone. She had roughly sheared her own hair when Ninj A'PaTa died, a grief tradition that we all practice, especially with the loss of a husband. Slowly, her will to live returns. Her mother and daughter still need her. This new life within her quickens and begs for breath. She is proud of Ninj A'PaTa, knowing he died bravely, as befitting a Chief and warrior. She will tell her unborn child about the bravery of his father; she is convinced this baby is male.

When the time comes to give birth, we continue to work at whatever job we were doing on that day; be it planting, weeding, or harvesting, wood gathering, cooking, and so on. We have learned from observing laboring animals to control our breath during the tightening, to help manage the pain. We view childbirth as a natural part of life; it is not to be feared. Once contractions are close together, the pregnant woman goes near the vicinity of the Blood House and is joined by the tribal midwife. If the weather is mild, labor takes place outside in the fresh air, the mother-to-be walking between the pains. The midwife is prepared with a sharp shell for cutting and hemp twine to tie off the cord. She has mats and supple tanned leather for wrapping the baby and mother together once the birth is complete. The midwife creates a soft bed of leaves where the mother will squat to push her baby out into the world. Xo has been trained as a midwife by her mother, KeSaTo, who was trained by her mother. Their family has been a part of the healing practices in our tribe for many generations. One of Xo's uncles is now a priest and oversees the diagnosing of illness and the prescribing of medicinal herbs. Because we don't consider childbirth an illness, the healing priests do not get involved unless the mother or baby dies.

Xo has already declared she will labor and deliver alone, as her mother is too sick to attend. While WaBus has assisted both her mother and grandmother in other births, at ten winter moons old she is still a child, too young to bear the full responsibility of guiding new life into this world. Xo's grief is making her irrational about this, but there is plenty of time to talk her into having someone in attendance when her time comes.

Ah'SaWei
(Golden Fawn)

It is the time of C*oHatTaYough*, Planting season in Virginia. As it is every spring, when I lie down on my sleeping platform, I am exhausted and yet, content. I wait for my man, MaMan, to join me. I know he is talking with my brother outside our dwelling. It is quiet while I wait; I hear the faintest crackle of the dying embers from the fire pit in the middle of the room. It is not for heat at this time of year, but to keep away mosquitos. The charcoal remnants will be used to restart the outdoor cooking fire in the morning. I hear the soft snoring of my mother, sleeping on the far platform. She cradles my toddler daughter, MaNa, in her arms. She has covered them both with a deer hide, even though it is late spring. I tease her about getting old and cold; she has seen forty-two winter moons.

The flap of the door lifts, and I see my husband's silhouette as he walks toward our bed. A glint of illumination from the night sky shines through the opening on the ceiling, highlighting his glistening body, the walnut oil I painted on him this morning still visible. I extend my hand, so he knows I am awake, and he lies beside me. We face each other, smiling and comfortable. I have known him my whole life and we were married shortly after my first blood, when I had seen fourteen winter moons.

He gently rubs my nose with his nose, and then my cheeks and neck. He knows I like it. I caress his head, noticing the stubby growth on the right side. I remind myself to shave it for him tomorrow. I pull the dried crow's foot out of the knot of hair on the left and the bound-up braid unfurls across his shoulder. We mate, on our sides, our sounds unnoticed by our slumbering family. We fall asleep to the chirping of the frogs and the quiet hooting of a nearby owl.

I sleep soundly, MaMan's body curled around mine. I wake up hearing my mother stoking the fire and carrying a small flame outside to start cooking for the day. The dried corn I put in the earthen pot last night with water to soak and soften is ready to be boiled into hominy for our morning meal. Our daughter, MaNa, climbs onto our platform and nestles between us. She picks up her father's braid and uses the end to tickle my ear.

We named her MaNa'AnGwa, which means Butterfly because she was so fragile and small when she was born, her skin translucent such that I could see her veins, but she was beautiful, just like a butterfly. She is still petite, like me, but feisty and strong-willed. She's hungry and pulls at my breast. My milk is drying up, but she suckles one side and then the other; it will tide her over till after we bathe.

Outside, our hamlet awakes. The dogs are stirring, sniffing for scraps to eat. The men head in the direction of the eel traps. The grandmothers begin to cook for the day. I gather two of our woven mats, take hold of MaNa's hand and we walk in the direction of the creek. Other members of our tribe are already washing, mostly women and children. We walk into the cold water and acclimate quickly. Clinging to my back like a baby opossum, MaNa makes a game of keeping her head above the water while I swim a little deeper. It is cold, but we are used to it; we bathe every day regardless of the weather. I stand in the deep and rinse my hair. Holding my daughter, I tilt her back into the water. Her head is bald except for a growing tuft at the nape of her neck. We keep our children's heads shaved until first blood for the girls and *HusKaNaw*, the rite of passage, for the boys. It helps keep the lice at bay. She smiles at me as she floats, knowing my hands will always be there, supporting her.

We climb from the creek, clean and energized for the day. I wrap MaNa in one of the mats to dry and wrap myself in the other. We join the prayer circle, already in progress. It is fluid; our tribal members will join and pray, offer tobacco to our God and then go about our work. I raise my hands in prayer toward the sun and look at the sky, hoping to see the mighty *ManGoi WeKoHis*, the Great Hare, creator of the PaTow'O'Mek. I do not see him in the clouds today. MaNa raises her hands and eyes to the sky, imitating me. We also offer prayers to O'Ki'Us, the God who oversees everyday life.

I pray silently for energy to plant much corn and for the health of each family member and the tribe. I pray for plentiful eels and fish, *CoHatTaYough* being a time of Hunger as we plant. The men do not hunt during the time of planting and growing, giving the animals time to birth and grow their young. We look to the river for fish, clams, crabs and eels to sustain us. If O'Ki'Us grants it, we will still have dried corn from the last harvest that will be ground into meal or soaked and boiled for porridge.

Not all petitions are silent. I hear the urgency of spoken prayers to keep the Strangers away. These Strangers have appeared in their flying boats for many years, gliding up the Potomac River. Our ancestors told us of the first ones, foul-smelling men from Spain. We do not know "Spain." Over time, we understood that the ones from Spain, with their heavy long robes, were from God, not our Great Hare or O'Ki'Us, but another God. They were ignorant and did not understand planting or fishing, so we fed them and took them in.

When they were our guests, we gave them companions for sleeping, clean and painted with fragrant oil, our way of showing hospitality. They could never be satisfied and took our women by force. The Spanish priests with their rancid breath and unclean privates abused us anyway. O'Ki'Us heard the prayers of our ancestors, and the Strangers from Spain left us, and there was a time of peace. Their temples rotted and returned to the earth.

Now we have new Strangers from England. Our elders tell stories of the arrival of the English Strangers. They came to us starving and begging for food sixty or so winter moons ago. They also stink; they rarely bathe, their breath and teeth repulsive. They are hairy and filthy; they cover themselves with woven layers, fetid with sweat and dirt. But they laugh and try to understand our words; they try to communicate with us. They, too, are always hungry, and we keep them alive, giving corn but also trading for glass beads or copper pots if they offer. We have recently started bartering for cloth and articles of clothing.

We do not trust them; they have killed many of us with their thunder sticks. We have killed them, too, when they invade our living spaces. They have caused more trouble for the southern tribes, near the mouth of the Potomac at the Chesapeake Bay, pushing those tribes out of their land by force and killing.

Our former paramount Chief Powhatan once asked them, "Why do you take by force that which you may have by love?"

But they are insatiable. Like lice, they keep coming and overtake everything. Our daily prayers now are, "Great Hare and O'Ki'Us, remove the Strangers from us, let us live in peace as did our ancestors."

MaNa and I leave the prayer circle and walk toward our camp. Several men, including MaMan, run to join us. He displays a spear loaded with impaled eels, and a basket of fish, still alive and gasping for breath.

I smile at my husband. "You had a good morning, did you?"

He is so transparent when he is happy, beaming with pride over the catch; we will not be hungry today. The spear with the eels is laid between two forked branches above the fire, to the side of the simmering pot. They will roast as we eat our hominy. My mother serves the porridge in bowls made of hollowed-out, dried gourds. We drink our morning meal with thanksgiving.

"MaMan, after you eat, I will shave your head and groom your face; come, now, when you are ready," I say.

There is no need to rush, although we need to get the corn and bean fields planted. I gather my sharp mussel shell for shaving and the crab claw for plucking and wait for MaMan outside our house. He saunters to me, we rub noses and he sits before me, ready to be groomed. The new growth is not overly long. The men keep the right sides short so the hair does not get tangled in the bow when hunting. I like caring for him this way, even if he could have waited a little longer. I rub some water on the bristles and carefully shave his head, starting above his right ear. The mussel shell is naturally sharp, but I honed it on our community whetstone to shave him without any nicks. After his head is smooth, I inspect his face for growth. His beard is sparse like all of our men. I do see a few emerging whiskers and using the crab claw as a pincher, I extract them and send him to the river to bathe.

My mother will tend to MaNa while I am away, planting with the tribe. She is already gutting and scaling the fish so they can be added to the pot, for stew we will eat later in the day. The eels will not be added to the stew; we eat them roasted separately. MaNa runs to her, and I wave goodbye to them both.

Before I walk to the field, I gather a pouch with dried seed corn and put on a simple leather apron that covers my loincloth. It is merely a tanned hide with an opening cut in the middle that I put my head through. The bottom is fringed, the movement of the leather strips helps keep the mosquitos away when I am walking. I secure it around my waist with a long piece of braided hemp, tied as a belt. I dip a feather in the vat of walnut oil mixed with pucoon dye and paint my arms, legs, and face. It is a daily practice in our tribe that helps to keep us warm in the winter and also repels mosquitoes and other insects in the warmer seasons.

The cleared fields lie about a mile away. We cultivate them by chopping down the smaller trees and burning off the underbrush.

We work around any larger trees that have fallen on their own, allowing them to decompose and become earth again. We have been planting corn, beans, squash and pumpkin seeds for two days. We plant together, the men and women, but after that, just the women will tend to the fields, weeding, harvesting, cooking, drying and storing the produce.

As I pass by the house of Xo, I call out, "*WinGaPo!* Greetings!" to see if she has left.

She calls back to me, "*WinGaPo!* Come in, Ah'SaWei, I just have to get the baby and make sure my mother is settled."

I lift the door flap and go in. Xo has her baby boy tied to the cradleboard and is hoisting him onto her back. She has lived twenty-six winter moons, and he is just her second living child. The first one, WaBus, is her daughter who will stay at the camp to care for her unwell grandmother. Between WaBus and this youngest boy, there were two boys who came too early and died at birth. I look around the room; all our dwellings are similar. The fire pit smokes lightly. WaBus kneels beside her still grandmother, stroking her graying hair.

Xo says to WaBus, "Be sure your grandmother eats a little bit and help her go outside for toileting." She walks over to her mother and daughter and touches each of them on the head, then she turns to me, and we start to hurry along the path to the field.

I am often struck by her beauty. Xo looks like her dying mother and yet different. She has flecks of green in her light brown eyes—no doubt a remnant passed from the Stranger who raped KeSaTo so long ago, impregnating her. Even though Xo is older than I am, we have been close since early childhood when she would often watch out for me when the bigger children were teasing or playing rough. Her hair has grown back from her period of mourning and is braided, keeping it from getting tangled in the cradleboard. A few lighter colored wisps have escaped around her face, giving her an ethereal look.

"My mother's stomach hurts today. She does not want to eat; her belly is swollen but her legs and arms are so thin," Xo says.

Her mother's abdomen has been getting larger for at least six new moons. The holy man has tried treating her with *PipSisSeWa*, a medicinal herb that sometimes helps with this type of growth. He has also painted her belly with paste made from boiled healing leaves, but the mass keeps growing and now she is getting weaker. We have seen this illness in our tribal women before. Sometimes it appears in the breast and ultimately the growths will break through the skin. I have known and loved Xo and KeSaTo since I was a baby myself. We are quiet with our thoughts as we consider what the future holds for her, and how long she will suffer with pain. We will talk about it privately when we are secluded in the *Mesk YiHaKan* during our monthly time of bleeding.

About twenty people, adults and teenagers, are at the field, busy with planting. Two babies, tied securely to their cradleboards, are suspended by leather cording in a large walnut tree. Xo carefully places her baby's cradleboard on a limb close to them, allowing them to see each other for comfort. Xo has the dried green bean and squash seeds, so we trade, mixing them together. We plant corn, beans and squash in the same hole, so the bean plant can use the cornstalk as support, and they will grow in unison. The squash grows low to the ground and helps preserve the moisture in the earth. Since the ground has been prepared for the past few weeks, it is soft and easy to dig the holes, drop in the seeds and cover with dirt.

We work about three feet apart, making our way down an unplanted area. When we come to a trunk or fallen tree, we just plant around it. Our planting tools are sturdy sticks, four hand widths long, with a piece of sharp, curved bone tied to the base. The English Strangers have said our way of planting is nonsensical. They like to completely clear the land and plant in straight rows. Yet, their crops often fail, and they come to us for corn when they are starving. We do it this way so after the harvest the Earth can more naturally replenish itself. We will find another field for the next planting season. We observe the English using the same field over and over again, each time enlarging the boundaries, but we know that ultimately the plants will not be healthy if the Earth is not allowed to rest.

Xo and the other mothers of infants take breaks to nurse their babies, sitting in the shade of the walnut tree. I stay in the field planting. The sooner we finish, the sooner we can get back to our village. I hear the men murmuring about rumors that the Strangers' chiefs of Virginia have been meeting in Jamestown. The English chiefs call themselves the Governor's Council. I overhear bits and pieces.

"We will not accept their appointed Chief. It is not our way. ... they do not remember how we gave them food. ... how we have tried to live in peace. ...they want more and more. ...they don't own this land ... the Earth is not for sale ..."

They have been asking us to sell our land for a long time now, but we will not do it. We have heard what happened to southern tribes when they agreed to share land with the Strangers. They were then killed or forced to move inland, away from the rivers and the bay that provided sustenance. We, the PaTow'O'Mek, are a proud people and do not want to leave the land on the Potomac River where we have lived for many moons, as did our ancestors before us.

By early afternoon we have planted all the seeds, and we start back to our hamlet. We pass a fallow field we had planted two years ago. It overflows with flowers and greens we can eat, as well as wild strawberries and onions.

I say to Xo, "Go ahead. I want to pick these wild onions and some strawberries for later. MaMan and MaNa love strawberries."

"I'll wait," she says, "I'm starving! I'll nurse the baby while you gather—but bring me some first!" She chuckles as she plops down and swings the cradleboard toward the front of her body. She loosens the straps. Her baby roots around for her breast. He is hungry, too. I remember being constantly famished when MaNa was a baby and how all the other women made extra effort to feed me, so my milk would be plentiful and rich, my baby strong. I easily fill my empty seed pouch with strawberries, take them to her and pour them out in a mound on the ground next to her.

"Eat!" I say, laughing, and go back to forage for more, and also to gather onions that will flavor today's pot of stew. When I have filled both our bags and can carry no more, I return to sit with Xo while the baby finishes feeding. He is plump and healthy, and I admire him with loving eyes. I, too, would like another baby, if the Great Hare is willing. With my tongue, I slowly mash a strawberry against the roof of my mouth. It is warm from the sun, the juice sweet and satisfying.

"Mmmmm, so good," I say to the sky and pick up another.

As we sit, another work crew comes into view. They have been gathering wood to keep the village fires going. We rotate jobs within the tribe. Gathering wood is my least favorite assignment, but it is necessary to keep the flames alive in the individual dwellings and for the community cooking fires. Each member of the crew is loaded with kindling, larger sticks and logs, tied in bundles, strapped to their backs. Two dogs trot beside them.

"*WinGaPo*," we say as they pass.

Our village is bustling as we approach. The crew that worked the fishing weirs collected a larger than usual catch, and some of the smaller fish have already been prepared for drying so we can eat them during the next moon. The fish are arranged in a single layer on a finely woven net, underneath an awning to protect them from marauding birds. Men loiter around the fire, eating roasted eel and fish as fast as they are cooked. The grandmothers, including my mother, scowl and scold them for eating everything too fast, but it is playful teasing. We are always so happy when food is plentiful, and we eat with gusto. Two large pots of stew simmer with fish and dried corn. I hand my mother the satchel filled with onions.

"Ah, very good!" she says, and brushes off any remaining dirt, dips them in a bowl of water for cleaning and then begins to cut them directly into the pot. The stew smells delicious.

We eat outside this evening, small groups of women and children together, while the men segregate themselves. We will eat all the stew and roasted fish and eel. Nothing will be wasted. If a morsel drops to the ground, one of the dogs will snatch it up.

Every evening after dinner, we dance and sing as a tribe. It helps us relax and brings joy, as these are the dances and songs passed down from our ancestors for many generations. The rhythm of the drums mirrors my heartbeat and I take a deep breath. I notice the warm breeze on my face and I want this moment to last forever. I stand and join the other women in the moving circle; MaNa runs to me, taking my hand. We move to the right, our feet softly pounding the dry earth. A light coating of dust settles on our feet as we dance. These dances are so deeply ingrained, we never count the beats, our bodies move fluidly as we change direction and dance to the left. I see Xo and WaBus on the opposite side of the circle and we smile at each other. Xo is a head taller than everyone else. My heart fills with affection looking at her. I hope that our daughters will be close just as we are even though WaBus is older than MaNa by seven winter moons. WaBus starts laughing, her eyes on MaNa.

When I look down at my daughter, she is making a silly face and sticking out her tongue. This makes me laugh, too. Our life is so comfortable; I don't want it to change but trouble is brewing. We all feel it.

The Strangers have harassed us for so long. They have tried to trick us and buy our land, kill us and take our land. They even arrested our Chief and charged him with murder and treason. Colonel Guilford, the porcupine, was involved in making the false charges. We know that at the trial our Chief was found innocent of the charges and released, but he never made it back to us. We heard that one of Strangers testified that Guilford had actually killed the four men and tried to cover the crime by blaming Chief WaHanGaNoChe.

Colonel Guilford was then fined for issuing a false warrant, but he was not charged for the murders.

In spite of the mistreatment, we remain firm and steadfast; refusing to acquiesce. The men constantly discuss what to do next. Chief WaHanGaNoChe has been gone, missing, and vanished for many moons. He disappeared without a trace after the trial. The men review this mystery frequently. I hear them, recounting the story as they know it, pondering what they do not know. The interim chief, his brother Ninj A'PaTa, was murdered, that we know for sure; we have his body. We are holding onto hope that Chief WaHanGaNoChe will miraculously return.

MaMan is speaking loudly to the other men. "Brothers, we must make a plan. It has been many moons since Chief WaHanGaNoChe was taken to trial in Jamestown, accused of murdering four of the English Strangers. We knew this was a lie. Chief WaHanGaNoChe believed we must form a partnership with the English and even allowed two of his daughters to marry Strangers of high rank to build a political bond that would help preserve the tribe."

Everyone knows this, but it is repeated often as we seek to understand what happened.

He pauses, and no one interrupts him. The women stop their dancing and are listening now, too.

"We know he was found innocent because shells, beads and tobacco were brought to us on his behalf as compensation and atonement for the false charges. The Strangers who accused our Chief had to pay a penalty for their lies, the Stranger's King demanded the restitution."

MaMan pauses, thinking before continuing. "We know WaHanGaNoChe was making his way back to our village, Colonel Guilford even told us he was released after being exonerated—but he never arrived." MaMan's voice gets quieter as he speaks, pondering his own words, hoping for new insight but the facts remain the same.

As he draws a breath to continue, my brother, A'KwiMex, interrupts. "Enough! Enough! It is time for revenge! Stop pretending that WaHanGaNoChe is coming back! We have heard the rumors that he was killed. And we know without a doubt his brother Ninj A'PaTa was tortured and mutilated while serving in his place, awaiting his return. We found his disfigured body. His bones lie decomposing in the temple as we sit here."

My brother has the reputation of being quick tempered, but I have known him all my life, and underneath the bluster, he is solid and dependable.

"The English did not even honor their silver badge of protection given to WaHanGaNoChe by their King Charles to guarantee his safe passage back to us! The Porcupine told us about the silver badge given by their King that would allow safe passage. So many lies. They cannot be trusted. They don't even honor the mandates of their King. The charges against WaHanGaNoChe were a sham. We refused to sell our land, and the English framed our Chief for murder—so they could take our land as retribution. It was so obviously fraudulent that *their own tribunal* found WaHanGaNoChe innocent of the charges!" His voice is filled with emotion as he recounts the same story my husband just told.

The retelling incites the other men to stand and join him in chanting, "Revenge, revenge, revenge!" The pent-up anger boils over, finally voiced in words. The women have known it was coming; we wanted retribution as well. We are tired of the abuse and seeing our people killed and accused of wrongdoing.

We, the PaTow'O'Mek, had resisted joining the attacks in 1622 and 1644 that killed so many Strangers. We had helped them when they were hungry and cold. Is it now time to rise up against our enemy? Will we be a part of a revolt against our tormentors this time, maybe even lead the charge? If we do not, our tribe will be decimated like the southern tribes, and we know it. We struggle with our contradictory thoughts, because the PaTow'O'Mek are known as a peace-loving, cooperative tribe.

From somewhere deep in his being, MaMan lets out a chilling howl that silences the calls for vengeance. "We are of one accord.

We will bring offerings to O'Ki'Us and wait for a vision and a plan, then we will act. We will anoint a new Chief even as we await WaHanGaNoChe's return. It is settled."

As he sits, the standing men follow his lead. We cannot deny that something has changed.

Our bowls and utensils are cleaned and put away now. Our dancing was cut short due to the emotional discussion but now we gather our musical instruments to dance before sleeping. We move in formation: the outer circle of men, the inner circle of women, moving in opposite directions, keeping the rhythm with our feet and the percussion from the drums, rattles and reed flutes. KeSaTo, who had been a talented dancer in her younger days, is now too weak to stand for very long, so she sits outside the circle on a mat with a small drum. She starts the first song.

"When Spirit speaks, we listen.

When Earth speaks, we listen.

It is so, it is so.

When Spirit calls, we follow.

When Earth calls, we follow.

It is so, it is so."

While her timing is still impeccable, the beat is light and her voice breathy and soft. The song is a lament, and we all join in singing and moving like a wheel within a wheel. I wonder, is she mourning her own death or is this choice of song about the tribe?

Tears fall from her eyes and another song is started, this time a song of praise to O'Ki'Us for his protection. The song is more upbeat, and our dancing becomes more animated, with solo dancers moving to the center and then stepping back into the circle. The words are repeated several times, with harmonies as more join in to sing.

"Praise to you, O'KiUs.

We offer, we bring.

Tobacco from your bounty.

We offer, we bring."

After that, we sing a playful, irreverent song about the unclean ways of the Strangers that transitions into a war song, the emotions from the earlier discussion not forgotten but amplified and now put into a call for action. The dancing becomes a frenzy of movement and exaggerated gyration, with loud exultation and calls for bravery and dignified death, if that is what it takes. We dance until we see the moon high in the night sky and the stars are shining. The moon and the stars are not worried about the Strangers; they sparkle and glow as if nothing is wrong at all.

Exhausted, we make our way to our dwellings, the women walking together, holding the hands of the younger children and cradling sleeping babies. MaMan and A'KwiMex walk together, discussing the next steps.

"We have to get the neighboring tribes involved," my brother says. "We have to be unified if we attack. If the Strangers do not suffer extensive losses, they will return and seek vengeance on us. We cannot undertake this raid lightly." Although my brother is intelligent and an excellent hunter, he struggles to control his temper. His temper is softened by his mischievous side.

My husband is listening, his head bowed as he walks, deep in thought.

In our tribe and other tribes in Virginia, it is common for our names to evolve or change completely over the course of our lives. It is especially true for the men. A new name is always bestowed after *HusKaNaw*, the rite of passage that describes their personal transition into manhood. Now, after twenty winter moons, my brother's name has recently changed for the third time to A'KwiMex. It means Crazy Fox—because he is funny and unpredictable, smart as well as stealthy. He is admired for these traits.

My husband and brother whisper together as they walk, and I can no longer hear what they are saying. I remember when A'KwiMex returned with the other boys after completing their rite of passage. They had been gone for six moon cycles, secluded in the forest, transforming into their roles as adult men in the tribe. There was always fanfare and celebration when the boys returned as men. All the newly anointed men were painted red or black or yellow and adorned with the pelts of deer, raccoon, fox and beaver. On their heads they wore crowns of deer antlers, dried whole crows and elaborate feather headdresses. A'KwiMex led the parade back into the village. He had indeed grown while away for *HusKaNaw*. He was taller and suddenly regal and yet, even then a prankster. For in addition to his fox-fur mantle and deer head with antlers crown, in one of his earlobe piercings, instead of the usual shell and bone earrings, he had inserted a live thin green snake about the length of a forearm. The snake's head was weaving around A'KwiMex's face and mouth as he walked toward us, appearing to kiss my brother! We all started laughing when we saw it and I smile now, remembering that happy day.

We say our good nights, watching as my brother continues on to his dwelling. He lives with his wife's family a few houses from ours. MaMan and I lie down together, depleted from the intense dancing and the rumors of war. I can tell his spirit is troubled. His eyes are closed, and I gently place one of my hands across them.

"Sleep, husband," I whisper. With the thumb of my other hand, I slowly stroke the middle of his forehead upward. "Sleep," I hum to him.

As he settles, I turn and snuggle into the crescent of his body, relishing the comfort of his warmth but sensing that the rhythm of our lives was going to be disrupted in the near future.

Ah'SaWei
(Golden Fawn)

It is later in *CoHatTaYough*, the planting is complete and now we concentrate on weeding the fields to keep the crops healthy. O'Ki'Us has sent rain and the plants are growing well, but it is too soon for harvesting. Our stores of dried corn are gone. Now we must forage for tuckahoe, a tuber that grows in the water. It will sustain us until harvest time. Tuckahoe is difficult to acquire, as we have to dig down in the mud with tools or our toes to extract the plants from their robust underwater root systems. Once we dig up the tubers, they need to be cleansed of clinging mud, stripped of roots and rinds, before being put in the bottom of the canoe. They ooze a substance that stings our flesh, so we work quickly to avoid prolonged exposure to our hands and feet. When we get the harvested vegetable back to our hamlet, we dry it in the sun or bake it. After it is dried, we pound it and use it as flour or meal, the same way we use dried crushed corn for bread and as a thickening agent in stew.

Today we will take two canoes to find the tuckahoe. I am in the first canoe, my mother, who we call *Nek*, my brother and my husband. MaNa is too young to harvest tuckahoe, so she is staying behind to play with other children while we work. The second canoe has four people as well, including another grandmother. After years of experience, the older women are experts and can quickly prepare the tuckahoe as it is pulled from the water. My mother insists the tuckahoe secretions do not sting her hands and feet anymore; she has calluses from years of hard work, but I do not believe her completely. I think she enjoys being out on the water and being productive and helpful, especially doing a job no one relishes.

We push the canoes halfway into the water before jumping aboard, and they gently float out into the river. It is peaceful this morning, the early summer sun already hot. I hear the quiet lapping of the water against the side of the vessel. I look at my mother. She has a small smile on her lips, enjoying the simple pleasure of the warm breeze on her face, which is raised to the sun. She realizes I am looking at her and smiles more brightly at me. We are alike in many ways and find great happiness with our life here on the banks of the Potomac.

But today, we have another mission in addition to collecting the tuckahoe. The men, led by A'KwiMex and MaMan, have been visiting nearby tribes for several weeks, enlisting support to take a stand against the Strangers who have been tormenting us for so many years, taking our land, and now, demanding to appoint our chiefs.

The PaTow'O'Mek have not accepted a chief from the Governor's Council. We are waiting for the return of our Chief WaHanGaNoChe. In reality, we are quite sure he is dead, but we have never recovered his body, so that is our excuse for refusing the Council's appointed chief. We have not forgotten the brutal way Chief Ninj A'PaTa was murdered. However, it is tricky and fraught with danger to approach other tribes to discuss action against the Strangers. While the appointed chiefs are from the various tribes, some have become traitors when given positions of authority and gifts from the Strangers. The Governor's Council is obviously hoping to curry favor and loyalty from those they appoint, a not-so-subtle way of keeping tabs on the tribes.

The best time to harvest tuckahoe is mid-tide. With low tide, the canoes get stuck in the mud and, with high tide; the depth of the water makes it harder to reach the roots on the river floor. We see a patch of the plants, the leafy heads swaying with the current, revealing their presence. When we get to the spot, the grandmothers stay in the canoes while the rest of us hop out and begin locating plant roots, following the stem to the place it is implanted on the river bottom. If we are unable to dig it up with our toes and hands, we have tools to loosen the roots from the earth. A'KwiMex always wants to be the first to pull up a tuckahoe plant, thus he makes everything into a friendly competition. To that end, he dives below the surface and when he emerges, he is holding a large plant.

"I am the king of the tuckahoe!" he announces with a laugh and tosses it to our mother in the boat. As she rises to catch the unwieldy plant, its roots spraying dirt and water, the canoe wobbles and threatens to spill her overboard.

She pretends to castigate him, saying, "Get busy, we don't have time for foolishness, A'KwiMex!" She is trying hard to look angry, but she is fighting back laughter.

We start concentrating and focus on filling the boats with the plants. The grandmothers admirably keep up the pace, cleaning and peeling the plants, readying them for drying. We will take some of the tuckahoe to the Portobacco tribe as a gift for their hospitality, allowing us to visit. After we gather the two boatloads of tuckahoe, one canoe will go back to our camp and the other will continue to the north side of the Potomac. We will visit overnight with the Portobacco tribe and hopefully enlist their support.

"*MaCaNuTu WinKan*, we leave each other well," we say to one another as we part ways, our canoes laden with tuckahoe. This is our traditional parting salutation. I am going with my brother and husband while everyone else is heading back to the PaTow'O'Mek village. Once we are underway, MaMan starts pondering how to approach the Portobacco chief.

We have known their chief for many moons, and he has always been quiet and unassuming. He had not distinguished himself among the Portobacco, and yet he was chosen by the Governor's Council to be their chief. He is called ToDoNoBo WeSKin, Milk Eye, because several years ago he became blind in one eye, his right eye turning milky and opaque seemingly overnight. Now he is Chief Milk Eye. The Portobacco accepted this appointment. We heard that in return, they were given many strings of pearls, copper bracelets and woven blankets.

"I do not trust Chief ToDoNoBo WeSKin," says MaMan. "But we need to know where he stands. We need to be united if we are to confront the Strangers."

Talking out loud, reminding himself and us, he continues, "We have support of the other neighboring tribes—the Nanjemoy, the Nanzatico, the Mattaponi and the Pissaseck. All are in agreement that the Strangers must be stopped before there is no land left for us and future generations. We cannot wait much longer. We need to be unified with a plan before the harvest is ripe or they will steal our corn again, as they have done in past seasons. Today, we will approach the Portobacco as allies, offering the tuckahoe as a gift while carefully observing not just Chief ToDoNoBo WeSKin, but his wives and the warriors who are providing his protection."

MaMan concludes, "If the Chief will not meet our gaze, we must be careful and not share our plans."

"Ahhh, easier said than done," jokes A'KwiMex, "as he has only one eye with which to look upon." We smile at his joke.

As we pull the canoe onto the northern bank of the Potomac, we spy ripe blackberries growing in a nearby thicket. We pluck and eat them right off the vines, careful to avoid being stuck by the thorns. I pick some blackberry leaves as we eat and store them in my satchel. Tea made with dried blackberry leaves aids with fertility and mating, thus they are helpful to have on hand. Beneath the bush is a large black snake, patiently swallowing a frog. We observe him and he seems to acknowledge our presence. We all keep eating without interrupting one another.

MaMan and A'KwiMex carry the woven basket full of tuckahoe between them as we approach the Portobacco village. The tribe also has a protective palisade surrounding their dwellings, similar to the one that protects our homes. The opening is unguarded and as we enter, MaMan calls out, "*WinGaPo*! Hello!" to announce our arrival. Several men approach; we recognize them, and they us.

There have been reasons to visit in the past and occasional intermarriages between our tribes. The men, in turn, call to some women, and they graciously received the tuckahoe, a welcome gift at this hungry time of year. It is safe to assume their supplies of dried corn have also been exhausted by this point.

It is late afternoon and we are invited to Chief Milk Eye's dwelling. It is dark and smoky inside as we enter. He is seated on a platform at the far end, flanked on each side by a young maiden. These are likely his most recent wives, acquired since he became chief of the tribe. He does not speak but motions to our escorts to prepare pipes for smoking, and we understand that talking will take place after that. He is an awkward fellow, the blind eye oozing pus that crusted on his cheek as it dried. It is hard to look at him, and we all notice that he will not maintain eye contact with us. We smoke in silence, passing the pipe between the three of us, the Portobacco Chief and his two teenaged wives.

When A'KwiMex can bear the silence no longer, he clears his throat to speak. Before a word can leave his mouth, Chief ToDoNoBo WeSKin lifts a heretofore unseen scepter and pronounces, "First, we will eat."

As guests, we maintain our silence and follow our host outside where a feast has been prepared. We fill ourselves with stew made of greens and oysters, there is fried bread, made from tuckahoe that had been previously dried and ground into flour, embedded with strawberries and walnuts. As our empty bowls are gathered, I know my brother and husband are eager to speak to the Portobacco chief and the whole tribe about the possible insurrection against the Strangers.

Again, the Chief speaks. "We will dance now." The Portobacco dance style is similar to ours but instead of a circle of men and a circle of women, the genders mix together. Two circles move in opposite directions, but males and females dance in both. They sing as we join the dancing, but the songs are unfamiliar. Chief ToDoNoBo WeSKin does not participate; he merely watches with his one good eye.

At last, we sit around the communal fire. The time has come for dialogue.

MaMan begins. "Thank you, great Chief ToDoNoBo WeSKin, for the hospitality you have shown toward your PaTow'O'Mek brothers and sister. We are grateful to have shared this time with you."

He hesitates slightly and then says, "I will get right to the point. We wonder if you are concerned about the Strangers' desire to take more of the land along the Potomac River. The south side of the river has been encroached upon and there is less and less land for foraging and planting crops. How is it here on the north side for you?"

He pauses, trying to gauge the response. He has clearly chosen his words carefully in case the Portobacco do not concur. MaMan sits quietly, waiting for a reaction. He motions subtly to A'KwiMex, urging him to remain quiet and observant, as well. Sitting with silence is an acquired discipline and hard to perfect, but extremely effective when negotiating or determining where one's opponent stands.

After what seems an eternity, Chief Milk Eye stands and says, "We have not been unduly troubled by the Strangers here on the north shore of the river. Yes, they are arrogant and dirty, but basically harmless. If the PaTow'O'Mek are having a problem, I suggest your problem might be solved by letting the Governor's Council appoint your chief."

He looks toward the sky as he speaks and then leaves the circle, followed by his entourage. I feel the heat rising in my own face with this rebuke and I know that both MaMan and A'KwiMex are livid. We are shown to the guest house where a young girl is waiting, available for coupling and sleeping, should either man want a companion other than I. A'KwiMex is in no mood for a Portobacco partner and sends her on her way, although it occurs to me that it might have helped calm him down.

"Go to sleep, A'KwiMex; it is not safe to talk here," whispers MaMan. "We know where the Portobacco chief stands, and that is what we came to find out."

I am troubled by what we have learned and again have the sense of impending doom that our lives are going to change. MaMan and I cling to each other passionately and as we lie together, unexpected tears fall from my eyes. Exhausted from the tuckahoe harvesting, the emotional exchange with Chief Milk Eye and mating, MaMan falls into a deep sleep on the north shore of the Potomac River in the camp of the Portobacco people.

I want to sleep because I am also extremely tired, but sleep will not come to me. I lie still beside my husband, holding his hand as he slumbers, thinking about all the ways this could play out. There is no scenario with a good outcome. As a shiver runs through my body, all I want to do is hurry back to the safety of our village and hold my daughter close.

Ah'SaWei
(Golden Fawn)

We have heard a rumor and learn that the rumor is true—we will be forced aboard one of the flying boats and taken to a place far away, an island called Barbados. Before we board the boat, we are taken to a small tributary and allowed to bathe while the guards leer at us. It is disconcerting but tolerable, just to be clean once again. Being clean does not offset the anxiety about what will happen next. We are standing on the shore, looking out at the bay where several boats are anchored, bigger boats than we have ever seen. Then, in groups of fifteen, we are rowed in a smaller vessel out to the huge flying boat. There are four Strangers rowing, and we sit quietly, clinging to our children. Our stolen babies have not reappeared as promised. We are bereft and numb from our mounting losses—from the surprise attack that killed our husbands, brothers, sons, fathers and then the kidnapping of our babies. I look to the sky, hoping to see the Great Hare, praying that we will be rescued somehow, but I do not see Him in the clouds. There are no clouds today; the sky is clear blue. I wonder if the Great Hare has deserted us, withdrawn his protection.

I am in the second group, my little MaNa beside me. My mother has managed to be on this boat, too. When we get to the larger vessel, we have to climb a rope ladder to board it. My thoughts start to race. MaNa has not even seen her fourth winter moon. How will she manage and how can I hold her? One of the Strangers demonstrates how to climb the ladder and encourages us to hurry along and board the larger boat. I motion for others to go ahead, watching to see the level of difficulty. Another man is steadying the ladder where we grab onto it and begin. We are generally agile due to our life of foraging, hunting and fishing. The older children in our boat scramble up without any problem, as do the other women. I place MaNa in front of me, one arm around her, my other hand holding the rope and whisper to her.

"Don't be afraid my darling MaNa, I am right here, holding you. You will not fall, we will climb together, slowly." I have to be brave for her. My mother follows us in case we slip or there is some other unforeseen calamity. We ascend, measure by measure, until all three of us are at the top.

Once on the deck of the ship, we huddle together with the other women and children. It is hot. The wooden deck burns the bottoms of our feet, so we keep moving, little hops in place. My mother and I take turns holding MaNa, her young feet are too tender; they will blister if she has to stand.

We are stripped of our tunics and loincloths and must be examined, one at a time, while everyone on deck watches. The paramount chief of the ship is Captain Thomas. At first, he does the inspections of our bodies. He grabs our breasts, slaps our bottoms. He has us open our mouths while he peers in, looking at what? Our teeth? He occasionally laughs during the process and remarks to his assistant who returns the laughter. Other members of the crew are milling about, working with the ropes but also watching, sometimes sneering. We are used to being naked and take no notice of it ordinarily when we lived on the river in our village. This feels different, intrusive, and judgmental as we are pinched and prodded and our female parts exposed. Captain Thomas writes in his papers after each examination.

He eventually tires of this and the lesser Chief takes over. He is short and skinny; his breath smells of rotten eggs. He reports to another man who records the findings in the paper book. He is even more disrespectful as he inspects our bodies, inserting his fingers into our female parts, looking around, laughing to see if he has an audience. I hate him. We all hate him and he will regret this day, the day he violated our bodies.

We are assigned new names; we are never asked our real names. I am called *Twentynine*, they call MaNa *Twentyeight* and my mother's new name is *Thirty*.

The cruel lesser Chief, the one with the repulsive breath, pushes us toward the upper deck. The other sailors call him "Matey." I will not forget his name or his cruelty. As we approach, I catch a whiff of what smells like burning flesh; my mind flashes back to the night of the massacre when there was a similar odor in the air.

The women and children from the first boatload are lined up and led to a small fire, one at a time, where several Strangers are working together. The fire is contained in what looks to be a large copper pot. I have seen pots like this when trading with the Strangers, but they were used for cooking, not to hold fire. We are prisoners now and we will be marked as such. Each PaTow'O'Mek woman and child is restrained by two Strangers while Matey presses the red-hot iron on the side of one hip, burning the flesh in the shape of an angular tree branch. We learn later that this is the English letter T, indicating we are owned by Captain Thomas of the *Trinity*, a slave ship. We are marked as his property forever.

Some of our women resist physically but are easily subdued and branded. Our children cry from the pain, and thankfully we are able to console them. The boys over the age of ten are brave like their fathers and brothers and show no emotion. I know their resentment is just below the surface. They will never forget the things that have happened to their families and the tribe. The final humiliation we experience on this first day on the *Trinity*: Our captors cut off our braids close to our scalps. In spite of the heat from the sun, we are shivering as we stand on deck; naked, shorn and mutilated.

While we wait on the upper deck, I look back toward the land with its lush green trees, the clear blue sky and sparkling water; it is the only world I have ever known, *TseNaCoMoCo,* Virginia. My chest and throat become tight again, as they have so often in recent days, when I think about my husband and brother being dead. The tears spill down my cheeks as I try to breathe, and all I want is to be dead with them. As I struggle to regain my composure, mostly so MaNa will not be afraid, there is a sudden commotion.

The Strangers run to the side of the ship and look into the water to see what has happened. Some of us are close enough to strain our necks and try to discern what is going on. Amazed murmuring and whispers run through the remnant of our tribe standing on deck. Two women have jumped overboard off the smaller boat and are attempting to swim back to shore! I am proud of them for this act of rebellion, but immediately fear they will be drowned or killed some other way. It is hard to tell what is happening in the water, two of the Strangers jumped in after them and there is clearly a struggle, but all we can see is frenzied splashing. We are ordered to sit down on deck and cannot see how the drama unfolds.

It is early evening when all the surviving PaTow'O'Mek women and children are finally on board the *Trinity* and have been examined, given new names, had their hair cut off and their hips branded with the T. There was quiet talk throughout the afternoon that the women who jumped into the water were Xo and WaBus. When I finally saw them, their hair was still wet but they were alive and for that I was grateful. I knew immediately that Xo had jumped into the water in an effort to return to land, in order to find and retrieve her son. From this point forward, her will to live is fueled by the desire to reclaim her baby.

Our hips sting; the skin has begun to blister and swell from the burns. We are given bowls containing a thin soup made from corn, beans and rice cooked into a mush. It is not tasty, but it will sustain us. Then water is poured into the bowls for us to drink and we do so. What else can we do if we wish to live?

Captain Thomas joins us on the upper deck with several of the crew. He is speaking to us in English, and while we are beginning to understand more words every day, we do not know what he is saying, and no one is interpreting for us. He has his paper book and refers to it and then says in a loud voice, "Eightyfive!"

He repeats himself, louder each time, "Eightyfive, Eightyfive!" His eyes are scanning us as if he is looking for someone or something. "She's the one with the flower embroidery," he says to the crew who then begin to push through, roughly handling us to look at our backs.

Matey exclaims, "Eightyfive, here she is," and he takes her by the arm and pulls her forward to Captain Thomas.

Now we understand that Xo is Eightyfive, this is her new name. Xo towers over Matey; she could strangle him if she dared. WaBus tries to follow her mother forward even as the fear of the unknown shows in her face. She cowers behind a woman near the front.

We watch in disbelief as Captain Thomas binds her hands together with interlocking metal bracelets and locks the pieces with a key. He looks at the crowd of women and children and announces, "Manacles." As Eightyfive, our Xo, stands there, another member of the crew approaches holding a different kind of metal contraption that looks like two bracelets joined with a chain.

He hands the device to Captain Thomas and again, with a key, locks her ankles together and announces, "Shackles."

"Walk," he demands, looking directly into Xo's face. "Eightyfive, walk!" He repeats.

She doesn't understand so Matey gives her a shove from behind. As she tries to catch herself, she stumbles and falls, unused to the heavy shackles that impede her movement.

WaBus springs forward to help. "*Nek!* Mother!" she calls out and helps Xo to stand. They both now stand in front of the tribe, eyes downcast, naked and shorn, unsure of what to do or what will happen next. I can tell by Xo's expression that she will find a way, somehow, to make Matey suffer.

There is one more display of dominance. Captain Thomas pulls something from under his long coat; it has been tucked in his belt at the back, hidden. It looks like a wooden handle with many knotted ropes attached. The air seems to be sliced open as he cracks it on the deck. We all startle from the sound, with the realization that it is a whip.

Captain Thomas announces, "The Cat. The cat of nine tails." He snaps it across the deck once more, not quite as robustly. I feel my knees start to buckle, fearing he will use this whip on Xo. He is looking at her, trying to determine the level of her rebellious spirit; after all, she did jump overboard in an escape attempt.

Xo's spirit is strong and she now looks him in the eye, as she is his equal in height. He cannot hold her gaze. I look around at these women I have known all my life and I see fear, resignation and hatred in their faces. Some look nauseated and blanched, some holding hands with one another for solidarity and strength. We are strong, but how much more can we endure of this misery?

Captain Thomas appears to have a change of heart and unlocks the manacles and the shackles, handing them to his assistant. He coils the cat of nine tails and tucks it back into his belt, underneath his coat. He looks over the crowd once more, says something to the crew and walks to his cabin, intimidation complete.

Two Strangers herd us toward steps leading to the lower deck. They lift a grate off the deck and motion for us to go below. As we climb down the wooden ladder into the black abyss, the stench is overwhelming. It smells of death: the fetid odor a mixture of old urine, feces, vomit, sweat and blood that has impregnated the wood and dried into the planks where we are to live and sleep until we arrive at our destination. I have to blink several times for my eyes to adjust to the darkness so I can see. Toward the end of the room, there is a hole cut in the wood and beneath it, a large container.

The man points to it and says, "The necessary tub." We understand, this is where we will toilet. It is similar to the bucket we used when we were outside on the upper deck. The crewmember then calls out our new names; he wants us to lie in a specific order according to our names, which we now understand are actually numbers. We have been reduced to objects with no spirits or defining features. We are "One and Two and Three" and so on.

There is no room to stand; we must crouch to walk to our places and then either sit or lie down. The boards we walk on feel slimy. We are naked, our loincloths and tunics have not been returned. We find our spots; we are packed close together and the air quickly becomes rank and humid.

In the darkness, I am still, lying between my mother and MaNa. I reach for both of their hands and give them a squeeze. What kind of life is this for anyone, but especially this beautiful butterfly of mine? My eyes leak, and I turn onto my unburned hip toward my little girl. I stroke her hair and hum to her, hopefully providing some comfort. I rub her nose with my nose and then hold her with our foreheads touching. She has barely spoken since this nightmare began in what seems like a lifetime ago. The ship rocks back and forth, the sound of the waves trying unsuccessfully to lull us to sleep. We remain anchored in the bay.

Ah'SaWei

(Golden Fawn)

W e live aboard the *Trinity* for several days, anchored in the Chesapeake Bay, before starting the water journey. There is a lot of activity with smaller boats going to and from the shore, bringing supplies and barrels of food and water for the voyage. Containers filled with dried tobacco are being loaded into the hold beneath the upper deck. Toward dusk on the final evening before we are to set sail, a smaller boat approaches the *Trinity* with four African women on board, being rowed by some men we have never seen. The women are bound together by their necks in two groups with a device that constrains them, limiting their movement such that if one moves, the other was obligated to move in the same direction or they would both suffer.

I had never seen an African woman before. All the Strangers we had seen up to this point in our lives before the massacre had been white men. However, while we waited on board the *Trinity*, there were black men, slaves from Africa, helping to load the ship. When the black women got to the rope ladder, the neck restraints were unlocked and removed so they could climb up, one by one.

We watched with detached wonder as these naked women are poked and prodded by Matey, just as we had been, while Captain

Thomas records the findings in his paper book. As he puts his filthy finger into the mouth of one of the women to examine her teeth, she bites him!

Matey screams and yells words none of us understand, jumping up and down, holding his finger close to his body. He recovers quickly and slaps her in the face before biting her on the breast.

Captain Thomas finally intervenes saying, "That's enough."

Matey immediately moves away from the woman and says, "Aye, Captain, but she's a feisty wench, I'm just teaching her not to bite." He laughs and looks around, to see if anyone else is amused but no one returns his mirth.

Captain Thomas declares again, "Enough!"

Watching this degradation and being powerless to intervene was almost as bad as having experienced it personally, just days before. All four of them are badly scarred on their backs. It occurs to me that a device like the cat of nine tails had likely been used. The fire pit is prepared, and the T-shaped branding iron is heated. Captain Thomas calls out their new names and Matey now prods each one forward so they can be identified.

"Eightyseven, Eightyeight, Eightynine and Ninety."

Two of the crew approach Eightyseven and, holding her by the arms, walk her toward the fire. As the red-hot metal is pulled from the pot, she instantaneously begins screaming some unknown words in a high-pitched voice while simultaneously going limp and flopping to the deck of the ship right where she was standing. Her sudden change in demeanor alerts the other crew to hurry over and in the ensuing confusion, Ninety runs for the side of the ship and jumps over at the exact place she had just climbed up.

Most of the ship is rimmed with netting to prevent this kind of cargo loss, but this was the singular place, due to the ladder, where there was no netting. Those of us standing, captives and crew, run to the side of the ship expecting to see Ninety swimming away. Unlike when Xo and WaBus jumped over and began swimming toward shore, Ninety just completely disappeared, without a struggle at all. It seems that she has gone straight to the bottom, as if she was made of stone.

As we watched in silent awe, admiring her courage, the stillness broke, and the water became red and disturbed. It was clear that sharks had disposed of Ninety for good.

The other African women, Eightyseven, Eightyeight and Eightynine, offer no further resistance and their hips are burned with the T. Their hair was already quite short, so it is not cut again. Their resigned compliance is not enough for Captain Thomas, so after being branded, they are each locked into a pair of shackles. The rest of us watch helplessly as they struggle to keep their balance, adjusting to the rocking of the boat while having their ankles bound with the metal devices.

* * *

WHEN THE CREW PULLS UP THE ANCHOR the next day and we leave the shelter of the bay, the movement of the air is magnificent, and the ship seems to fly, the sails taut and full of wind. We PaTow'O'Mek women and children, as well as the three African women, sit or stand on the lower deck as we sail away from Point Comfort. Once we are significantly far from the shore, the African women are unshackled.

The African women understand English! The crew now barks orders to them and motion for the Africans to explain to us. With our eyes, we laugh together, knowing this is ridiculous: They don't know the PaTow'O'Mek language. Using pantomime, they gesture and repeat the English words, and we learn more words. "Sit" and "Go below" and "Eat" are the most frequent commands and we learn them. Although we do not know one another, being sold and transported against our wills unites us in spirit.

Captain Thomas is usually on the upper deck, safely protected from us by the barricado, the wooden wall that separates the upper and lower decks. Metal spikes are embedded in the wood at the top, preventing any of us from climbing over, lest we be impaled. There is a door in the barricado and beyond the door, steps leading to the upper deck. We are not allowed to trespass through the door or access the upper deck for any reason.

The crew, all men, work the sails with ropes and pulleys, some climbing the tall trees we now know are masts, adjusting and checking the fabric for tears or needed repairs. The climbers often carry a hollow wooden tube to peer out over the ocean to see if there are other ships nearby. Eightyseven says it is a spyglass and that it is magic, that the whole world can be seen through it.

When Captain Thomas wants to use the device, he says, "Bring me the telescope!"

Some men are assigned to guard us, standing watch with their thunder sticks, ready to discipline or kill us should we threaten revolt. Every man has a job aboard the flying boat.

We settle into a routine of sorts. We are packed into the suffocating hull from dusk to mid-morning. The necessary tub is in constant use; it is not sufficient for our numbers. It is unclean, especially compared to our tribal toileting habits: We would bury our waste in the woods and move from the used areas regularly, so no spot attracted vermin or disease. We learned this from our ancestors. The smell of the overflowing pot is nauseating. Often the children as well as the women are unable to hold their bowels or bladders, and the excrement falls on the boards just below the planks where we sleep. At first, about half of us suffer from seasickness, so vomit joins the mix as well. In time though, we adjust to the movement of the boat, and the queasiness from the motion abates as does the vomitus.

We emerge from our squalid tomb each day at mid-morning. Bowls of the corn, rice and bean mush are passed out, followed by water for drinking. We feel dirty and miss our daily baths in the river. Every few days, we are allowed, one at a time, to dip water from the rain barrel and pour it over ourselves in an attempt to get clean. It is not enough, but it helps. Then we sit on deck while the sun bears down on us, blistering our necks and backs. After we have been on the ocean for a few days, handfuls of glass beads are distributed along with cotton thread, and we string bead necklaces hour after hour. It is monotonous, but it gives our hands something to do and distracts our minds from our sorrow over our dead men as we try to create appealing patterns with the colors.

In the late afternoon, we are given another bowl of gruel and water. After that we are forced to "dance." The first night we are told to dance, a couple of the sailors try to demonstrate by doing a jig. I cannot help but smile, they look so foolish. When we do not immediately respond to the command, one of the men becomes enraged and asks for something from the upper deck and a cat of nine tails is thrown down to him. He viciously slices the air.

Eightyseven begins to move in a manner unknown to us but clearly her movements would ordinarily be accompanied by music of some sort. Eightyeight and Eightynine then begin to clap in rhythm and sing. This pleases the Strangers, and they motion for all of us to join in the dancing. Our movements are strained and contrived but we comply, no one wanting to experience "the cat." We dance in a circle, recreating our tribal dances but without the joy; this is only done under duress to avoid a beating.

Uninvited, Matey joins in, running in between us as we move. He slaps our bottoms as he goes by. When he passes by Eightyseven, she pretends to be a wild animal and snaps her teeth at him, threatening to bite him again. He was not expecting this and he is startled.

"Crazy wench." He mutters and walks away.

After the dancing, we retreat once again to the stinking belly of the ship, hoping for sleep and an end to this nightmare, which is our daily routine.

We are in the middle of nowhere when the wind stops blowing. All that can be seen in any direction is the ocean. Sometimes it is so still it looks like the glass we saw in the windows of the buildings at Point Comfort. Occasional birds fly overhead, and sometimes one will perch on top of the mast, apparently taking a rest. We have seen huge, strange sea creatures as well. We learn the largest ones are whales; they languidly pass us, oblivious to our presence and our predicament. They are graceful living things as they swim by and blow water from their heads.

Quite often we see groups of *Keit WijhCats NaMeChe*, the great fin fish. I had never seen them before, but my mother remembers seeing this kind of fish in the bay once when she was a young girl.

Captain Thomas is fascinated by them and calls out "Dolphins!" whenever they appear. We learn the sailors and captain consider their appearance as a good sign, a lucky omen that will bring the wind again soon.

The passage to the island proceeds slowly now. For many days the flying boat does not fly, it just floats and bobs, sitting in the big water, unable to move as there is no breeze. Captain Thomas and the crew are short-tempered about the lack of progress. They spend time putting the sails up and down, changing the ropes, trying to capture the air, but without success. During the daylight hours, we sit on deck, listening to the soft impotent flapping of the hapless wings, unable to do their job without the wind. The ship rocks gently from side to side on the water, and our bodies sway with the movement. We have gotten used to it.

* * *

I AM BEGINNING TO LOSE TRACK of the number of days and nights we have been aboard the *Trinity*. The first days went by in a blur as we learned what was necessary to survive and got used to the ship, Captain Thomas and the crew. Not realizing the wind could stop existing on the ocean, I paid no real attention to our progress in those early days, assuming the boat would continue to move toward our destination. No one actually said how long the trip would take, even in the best of circumstances. Thinking back, it does seem the wind was strong for many days, and then it slowed for a few days before it completely ceased. As the windless days linger, the crew becomes irritated, and we prisoners bear the brunt of their wrath.

All of us look much leaner than when we were captured. We are used to fluctuations in our weight, depending on the season and the bounty from the harvest, augmented with fish, eels, oysters, or meat from the hunting of deer and other game. We are familiar with hunger pangs but usually have so many options for sustenance with foraging always available. This gnawing hunger feels different.

It is obvious that the gruel is now being rationed, and we hear the crew complaining about their lack of food. Fresh drinking water is being conserved, and there is no water for bathing. I find myself thinking about death and wondering if I will die on this ship, out in the ocean away from the world I have known and loved. I know my mother is struggling with these same thoughts, but we do not speak of them. We know we must be alert and vigilant for MaNa to survive. My precious butterfly has not spoken for many days, she is listless as she clings to me and leans into my body. My mother and I both give her sips of our water and food to keep her alive. I am also watching out for Xo and WaBus. We are far apart when below in the hull due to our number names, but we try to stay near each other when above on the deck.

Xo sleeps near Eightyseven and tells me in whispered tones that Eightyseven wants all the women to rise up and take over the flying boat.

I look at Xo in disbelief. "We do not know how to move the sails up and down and there is no wind. The Strangers will kill all of us if we attempt such a thing." I look right into her eyes, so she understands without a doubt that I think this is a foolish and dangerous idea. She has always been bolder than I, but this is absurd.

She continues, "Eightyseven has been stealing pieces of metal and small tools that we can use as weapons. She has hidden them in the cracks beneath our sleeping platforms. She says when she was brought from Africa as a child on a similar ship, there was a mutiny and many of the Strangers were killed."

I look at her incredulously and shake my head, "*MaTa*, no. We cannot be successful. Many of us, or even all of us would die."

She has an odd, faraway look and the green flecks in her eyes are sparkling in the sunlight. As she stares at the ocean she continues, "If we kill some of them and get their thunder sticks, we can order them to return us to our land. I have to get back, Ah'SaWei. I have to get back to my son. I cannot live without him."

I am silent as I think, and she senses my reluctance.

"Don't be a coward, Ah'SaWei! Think about MaMan and A'KwiMex—how brave they were and how they were viciously killed," Xo implores. "Think about MaNa, our beautiful Butterfly. Do you want her to be a slave in this new place, this island somewhere? The Strangers where we are going could be even worse than these that we know."

When MaNa hears her name, she stirs from her lethargic state and looks at us. I draw her closer and rest her head in my lap. I do not want her to hear these disturbing words.

Xo will not be dissuaded. "When we get back, I will find my brother who was kidnapped so many moons ago. Remember the rumors that he works near our village on a farm? I will find him. He will help us find my son. I'm begging you, help us, Ah'SaWei!"

So many thoughts are running through my head. My mother was healthy when we were captured but she is not young. How can she fight these men? Neither of us has ever used a thunder stick. I do not know how to load it or how to discharge the fiery blast. But, then again, the idea of getting back and rebuilding our village tugs at my heart. I want to go home, too.

Even as the thoughts race through my mind, images of my husband and brother wash over me, and I have to choke back my tears. It suddenly does not seem so bad to die while attempting to take control of the *Trinity*. Daily it seems we are going to die anyway, likely by starvation or at the hands of the crew. Maybe we would capture the wind if we were going home; maybe the wind problem is a direction problem. For the first time in weeks, I feel a flutter of hope about the future.

I reach for Xo's hand and give it a squeeze. She looks at me and I nod my head yes in an almost invisible movement. She smiles and nods back. It is the first smile I have seen on her face since that horrible night in mid-summer.

Over the next few days, there is a discernible improvement in our attitude as we study the crew and Captain Thomas, deciding how and when we will attack. We want to keep alive only the ones who can sail and navigate; we will kill the youngest ones, the cabin boys and possibly Captain Thomas. We are quite sure the first mate knows how to manage the ship, so he will be spared. We despise him, but we have to be pragmatic. But Matey, the second mate, we hate even more. Who knows what his future holds. At night as we lie in the dark filth below the decks, we whisper instructions and plans. It is tricky because some of our tribe has been chosen to help prepare the daily food rations, and three women are taken to couple with Captain Thomas on rotating nights. We worry they might be tempted to reveal the plans, to save their own lives, but it is a chance we have to take. Our fates are tied together.

Eightyseven is the leader, since she is the only one who has been on a ship before and she speaks with experience, so we listen to her plans. It is decided that the older women, including my mother, will stay below in the hold with the children. The older boys will help us fight. Eightyseven is a wiry woman, thin but strong with big brown eyes and short tufted hair, like the feathers of a baby bird. It seems she never sleeps, talking to herself, thinking through the plans then crawling over each of us in the intimacy of the hull, showing us where she has hidden sharp pieces of metal and wood in the cracks and crevices beneath our sleeping planks. We will strike in the pre-dawn hours.

Xo helps explain the instructions, following behind Eightyseven, repeating the words in PaTow'O'Mek to be sure everyone understands, the most important lesson being that there can be no hesitation once the uprising starts. We must be single-minded and focused on killing at least six of the crew and controlling the others. Eightyseven plans to put manacles on the remaining crew until we are sure of their submission.

There is a total of twelve crew: eleven plus Captain Thomas. Matey is the only one who guards the lower deck now; the others sleep in their assigned berths, unless it is their turn to keep watch. Captain Thomas has his own private sleeping and eating quarters. There is also a Stranger standing guard every night on the upper deck, overlooking the sea and the lower deck, which includes the grate where we emerge and descend daily into our chamber. He is equipped with a thunder stick. There is consensus to act quickly once a plan is formulated. Eightyseven thinks that the crew is more inattentive because there is no wind and that our chances of success are better if we act with haste before they become aware of the talk of insurrection.

On the night we have decided to mutiny, we are given our scanty ration of watery mush which is followed by a few minutes of half-hearted dancing. I have no appetite; my stomach roils with nervous anticipation. Will we die tonight? The oblivious crew herds us below as always. As the moon rises and the boat slumbers, we stumble over one another, leaving our assigned places. There are twenty of us who will lead the first assault, and we gather in the spots closest to the grate. We are the strongest seventeen of the female captives, joined by three of the oldest boys. We each have a sharp object with which to do harm and kill, to protect ourselves as well as the children and older, weaker women who will wait below. I have a sharp piece of metal. It initially felt cold in my hand when

I pulled it from the hiding place beneath the planks where we sleep. It is warm now; I am gripping it so hard. The tip is sharp; I have to be careful, or I will cut myself as we wait. My heart is beating like a roaring river, I can hear it in my ears.

Xo finds me with her eyes and then crosses her arms across her chest, she nods, reminding me she loves me. Her confidence encourages and calms me. I am ready for this assault to begin.

The grate has not been latched since the wind ceased blowing, and over time, Eightyseven has perfected the art of lifting one side and peering on deck, checking the location of the guard, and seeing if he is awake. Tonight, it is Matey who is on duty.

Matey has fallen asleep and is some distance from the grate, so Eightyseven completely removes the wooden covering, climbs out and motions for us to follow. Like shadows, we emerge quickly and go to our positions, flattening ourselves against the wall of the barricado, the only place we can stand undetected. Simultaneously, Eightyseven and Xo creep over to sleeping Matey. Moving in unison as if they were one being, Xo covers his mouth and Eightyseven slashes his throat. They drag him over to the opening and throw him into the hold where he will be pulled into a corner and left to bleed out completely. He never knew what happened, it was so quick.

Now we wait until the guard on the upper deck notices his compatriot is missing and makes his move. It seems an eternity; the horizon is beginning to lighten when we feel a slight breeze. It feels so good; I immediately think O'Ki'Us is blessing our action and I silently thank Him and look to the sky. The breeze has also finally awakened the guard on the upper deck and he yells down to his missing sentry.

"Hey, wake up down there! Matey, get up, we have wind!"

It is tempting to step away from the wall and look up to see his location, but we make ourselves as flat as possible, hoping he will come through the barricado door, and we can kill him and take his gun.

We hear his boots on the deck, and he calls out again, but he is excited about the wind and comes stomping down the stairs, bursting through the door where we wait. He is thrust forward on his face, losing the grip on his weapon and it slides across the deck out of reach. For the briefest of seconds, I think Eightyseven hesitates but then in the blink of an eye, she reaches around his neck while he is prone and slits his throat from behind. His life flows from his neck like a red river. His dead body is pulled to the hole and emptied into it, leaving a trail of blood in its wake.

Eightyseven retrieves the gun and the rest of us scamper back to the protection of the barricado wall hoping to conceal ourselves for another minute. As Eightyseven stands in plain sight with the gun in hand she is suddenly shot from above and drops to her knees before collapsing in front of us. I am paralyzed seeing our leader, brave Eightyseven, slaughtered.

This is not what we had planned and while we had discussed some contingencies, losing Eightyseven immediately was not factored into those plans. We stand frozen against the wall and can hear the remaining crew running and shouting above us. At the same time, the wind picks up and we hear the voice of Captain Thomas joining the fray.

When the barricado door opens again, the four closest pounce upon the unfortunate sailor and in a frenzy stab him to death with picks made of metal and wood. This brings on a round of gunfire and those women are immediately killed. The remaining fifteen of us on deck are thrown face down and manacled with our hands behind our backs. We lay immobilized while the crew lifts the sails into place and the *Trinity* begins to briskly skim the water as the gale fills the wings.

Once the *Trinity* is under way, one of the crew drags the rest of the captives up on deck and they see us, shackled face down and helpless. I am horrified for MaNa to see me like this, and I know she will be afraid. I hope my mother will find the right words to comfort her. I know trouble is coming because of this attempted coup. The five women's bodies are quickly disposed of overboard. We are moving at such a brisk clip, no one knows if they were immediately eaten by sharks or not. One of the crew says a few prayers over the dead sailors; they are wrapped individually in fabric and thrown into the ocean, one by one, including Matey.

Eightyeight and Eightynine will suffer the most, their fate by association, simply because they are African and Captain Thomas is sure that Eightyseven instigated this rebellion. They were a part of the group of mutineers and so are pulled to standing and their manacles momentarily removed. They are then re-manacled to opposite sides of the mast. As everyone watches, they are viciously lashed from their necks to their knees, until their flesh is open and bleeding. They are barely conscious when the beatings cease but they are not released and hang limply, draped and falling from the mast.

The remaining thirteen of us that were found on deck receive two strikes each, which in essence equals eighteen bites from the cat. The three boys are flogged first and their backs open and begin to bleed with just two strikes. Xo is next and the stripes mar her floral tattoos, the flowers appear to be bleeding as she accepts the scourging without a sound. By the time it is my turn, the crew has begun to tire and while my back does open, it isn't as bad as the others.

We are returned to our assigned locations below decks with no food or water as another piece of punishment and a warning that Captain Thomas is willing to starve us if that is what it takes to keep us subdued.

Xo
(Shining Moon)

I lie on my side in the dark, stinking hull thinking about the failed mutiny. My back is bleeding from the lashing, the blood pooling underneath my body. The wounds throb and the blood is sticky as it dries. WaBus also lies on her side, facing me, eyes wide open, staring at me. We do not speak but I reach for her hand and hold it to my chest. After ten winter moons, she has more wisdom than is customary for a child. Her stomach is rumbling; she is hungry. We are all hungry. We were hungry before the mutiny.

I am filled with conflicting emotions. I'm angry because we failed and now, we continue toward the unknown island and an unknown future. Eightyseven was a slave; she explained what it was to be owned by another person. She told us we were all going to be slaves on this new island. There was no doubt about that. We knew we had been exchanged for gold when Captain Thomas took possession of us. She knew from past experience that slave owners did not want to lose any of their human cargo, and that Captain Thomas wanted to make a profit when he sold us in Barbados. Maybe she overestimated our value and thought none of us would be killed, just punished. This was part of the reasoning for the mutiny: We want to be free. We do not want to be sold again to a new group of Strangers.

I ask myself, do I regret what we did? I do not, but I am sorry that Eightyseven and four of my tribe members died. The days of planning and anticipation had been exhilarating. To have hoped to return to *TseNaCoMoCo*, Virginia, with WaBus and find my son—no, I do not regret it.

Eightyseven was fearless and her confidence was contagious. She was so fiery, so determined. In her, I saw a glimpse of my former self and it made me more hopeful and braver than I had been since our village was burned.

I cannot sleep even though the ship is moving along quickly now, and the rhythm is hypnotizing. WaBus has finally closed her eyes. I'm in a dreamlike stupor, maybe from the pain or the movement of the ship. I rouse when the hatch is removed and one of the crew climbs down into our fetid chamber. I do not move, but I watch him closely. He is trying to make himself appear big by puffing up his chest. It is gratifying to see that he is actually scared. He is afraid to be in the hold. I feel a smug satisfaction realizing this until he collects himself and starts yelling.

"Doctor, medicine, herbs, blood, sick. ..." He rambles on, making no sense. After a few minutes, there is murmuring from among the women and I hear my name being whispered, "Xo" and all the eyes turn toward me. Again, they murmur my name, and someone says, "Eightyfive."

Now the crewman bellows with assumed authority, "Come on, Eightyfive—now!"

I am dizzy as I try to stand, but I steady my stance and look at my daughter. I give a squeeze to my dear WaBus's hand. As I move past Ah'SaWei, my eyes tell her, "Take care of my child."

Once on deck, I follow him to the mast where Eightyeight and Eightynine lie together, unconscious. The Stranger motions for me to go to them. I place a hand on Eightyeight's heart. She is dead. I do the same to Eightynine. She is barely alive.

I look at the sailor as if to say, "What do you want me to do?" He looks to the upper deck where Captain Thomas is standing, scowling. I meet his gaze and our eyes lock, but he turns away, unable to look at me.

I follow the sailor who carries the nearly lifeless body of Eightynine into a small room near the cooking galley. She is laid out on the table and Captain Thomas enters the room. He gestures toward jars of spices, dried herbs and a barrel of water. Now I understand; I am to restore the health of Eightynine. I have been chosen for my knowledge of the healing practices in our tribe. The Captain and his mate leave me alone with my comatose charge.

Examining the jars with their cork stoppers, smelling the contents, rubbing the powders and leaves between my fingers, I try to identify each one. The jars are labeled but I do not understand the writing. I wash Eightynine with a wet rag and squeeze a few drops of water onto her cracked lips. I wish for walnut oil to massage into her skin but there is none. There is an oil that is fragrant in a different way. After smelling it, I taste it and find it to be an adequate substitute.

As I begin to rub the oil into Eightynine's feet and legs, a low moan escapes from her mouth. Perhaps she will live after all. One of the jars contains dried moss that looks like curly grey hair. I recognize it as *Mu'Xom MeSeToNans*, grandfather's beard. Our tribal priests used it to treat infection and to stop redness from developing in cuts. I make a poultice with the crushed grandfather's beard and oil, then I gently press the mixture into Eightynine's wounds.

Over the next few days, Eightynine begins to recover. I do not leave her side. We both sleep on the floor in the little room. As she returns to consciousness, she sits up, takes in the surroundings, and begins to talk. I listen closely and realize Eightynine is reading the labels on the jars. Eightynine knows how to read!

"Olive oil, pepper, ginger, cloves, cinnamon." She stops reading, looks at me and smiles.

I pick up the jar with the oil and hold it toward her.

"Olive oil," says Eightynine.

I repeat, "Olive oil." This is the beginning of my learning to speak and read English in earnest. We speak quietly as she teaches me the alphabet and words. If we hear footsteps approaching, Eightynine lies down and pretends weakness or sleep.

During our days together in the healing room, Eightynine tells me that she came to Virginia from Africa as a young child, kidnapped with her family and transported on a ship much like the *Trinity*. It had not been the same ship as Eightyseven; they had not known each other before boarding the Trinity and she had not experienced a mutiny. Upon arrival in the new land, she was separated from her parents and siblings. She never saw them again. She describes being sold and how her mother was screaming as they were being separated. She closes her eyes.

"I can still hear her cries in my dreams."

I think of my own mother, remembering how she was killed on the night of the massacre. I, too, still see her in my dreams.

Eightynine learned to read while enslaved, secretly learning the letters from another slave who could read. One day as she is teaching me, she points to herself and says, "Elizabeth."

I repeat the word, "Elizabeth." Her name is Elizabeth! Her owner had given her the name upon arrival in Virginia.

I point to myself and say, "NePa'WeXo."

She says, "NePa'WeXo" and we smile at each other.

A small token of humanity is restored with the sharing of names. A flood of feeling washes over me, hearing my name said in this way, by someone new, in the middle of the ocean on a slave ship bound for an unknown island. After everything, I am still NePa'WeXo, a strong PaTow'O'Mek woman. Her name is Elizabeth, she is not the number Eightynine. Captain Thomas's cruelty has not erased who she was, nor have I been weakened or destroyed. I remember my strength; I renew my own faith in myself. We lean toward one another, our foreheads touching, and then embrace. We both feel the power in this moment.

We continue this charade of sickness for several more days and enjoy the deception. We giggle like young girls as we play healer and patient whenever the door opens. But we cannot hide the fact that Elizabeth is getting better and indeed will live. Her eyes are brighter and the deep oozing wounds in her back are drying.

Captain Thomas orders us to be returned to the hold to continue the journey with the other captives.

Now every day after the morning meal, I am ordered to the little room where a steady stream of injured crew and the enslaved come to me for treatment. The sailors suffer from boils, cuts, infected splinters and other minor maladies. I assess the injuries, wash and dress them with a variety of concoctions, using olive oil as the base and adding the specific dried herbs or leaves as needed. Sometimes, I mix the herbs with water, heat the mixture in the galley and have my patients drink the healing teas.

Captain Thomas shows up at random times, watching me as I work. He has dark brown hair, a full beard sprinkled with some gray hairs. He walks with one hand resting behind his back. I assume he is confirming the whip is still in place. He is taller than I am, but not by much. He often scowls—maybe that is his usual expression, but sometimes, it seems he is wincing as I clean the captive's backs that were opened by the cat. He never says a kind word, though, so maybe I misunderstand his expression. I do, however, understand enough English by now to know that Captain Thomas wants the captives to look healthy upon arrival at the island, where he plans to sell us. Besides the cuts from the whippings, most of our ailments are skin issues from insufficient bathing and having to spend half the day in the humid, dirty hold of the ship.

I treat these problems as best I can. Their suffering from nagging hunger, and their broken hearts, I have no way to cure. I haven't been able to spend time with Ah'SaWei, her mother and MaNa since my daytime hours are spent in the healing room. At night we lie in our assigned, numbered spots, which prevents us from talking. WaBus assures me she is with Ah'SaWei every day and not to worry. Ah'SaWei comes as a patient to the healing room once. She does not need medical treatment but has come to check on me. Her back is healing well. The scabs made the snake tattoo on her back look like it was shedding its skin.

I chuckle when I tell her how it looks. "Ah'SaWei, your tattoo is getting new skin!"

She smiles. "Keep looking at my back while I talk to you. I wanted to make sure you were well and for another reason—something is not right with my mother. She is confused some of the time. She keeps saying we are on the way home, to *TseNaCoMoCo*. What will we do, what can I do for her in this new place, this Barbados island? I am worried about her. She doesn't appear well."

I answer her by saying, "Elizabeth told me her family was separated when they were sold; she never saw her parents or siblings again. We must stay together, no matter what happens. We will beg; we will do whatever it takes. If we are together, I can help care for your mother and we can protect our girls. We will be strong together, for WaBus and MaNa."

I am not sure I even believe my own words. Will it be possible to stay together? I want to comfort her, as I have always done. Ah'SaWei is younger than me, more petite, her disposition calmer while I am more impetuous. We are as close as sisters and I have protected her since she was a little girl. I am facing her back as we speak and I stroke the back of her head, feeling the soft new hair growth.

As she turns to leave the room, we part with these words, "*NihTe KihTe*', my heart, your heart." We both repeat the words; we love each other with all our hearts.

The wind continues to blow, and the slave ship *Trinity* moves toward the island of Barbados. We can feel the change in demeanor among the crew as we draw closer to the destination. Among the captive women and children, however, there is discernible anxiety; none of us have any idea what the future holds.

When they sight land via the telescope, the sailors let out a jubilant cheer. We captives watch in silence as the island comes into view. The sea is crystal clear, a shade of blue I had never seen in the waters of *TseNaCoMoCo*, the Potomac or creeks near our villages. The sun is hot on our heads and backs, but a breeze keeps it from feeling oppressive. Without warning, a sudden warm rain begins falling, washing off some of the filth from the past forty-three days. We all look to the sky, grateful for the water and cleansing.

We are on deck when the *Trinity* drops anchor in sight of the shore. We watch the crew lower a small dingy into the water with four of the men on board. The next hours are a flurry of activity as larger boats approached with barrels of water and other supplies. We bathe ourselves in preparation for the sale. While our hair is still wet, it is again roughly shaved off, eliminating the growth from the past almost seven weeks. For dinner, each of us receives a yellow and black fruit called a banana, in addition to a larger helping of gruel than we had been allotted since before the doldrums depleted the food stores.

The sailors are gleeful as they show us how to peel and eat the inside of the fruit. It is creamy and delicious, but we cannot really enjoy it, our fear of the unknown is so great. We wash it all down with a bowl of fresh water. Being clean and satisfied is a welcome change in circumstances. But not knowing the future is terrifying. Could it be worse than what we have already endured?

We march below for our last night on the ship, but no one sleeps, no one speaks. I hold WaBus's hand through the dark night. Elizabeth reaches over and pats my back. She hums an unknown song, and it soothes those of us who lie near her. She alone knows the horror of what awaits us.

The next morning the first mate instructs us to rub olive oil all over our bodies and our children's bodies. He gives us loincloths to put on for the first time since leaving *TseNaCoMoCo*.

On land, the sale is about to begin.

Ah'SaWei

(Golden Fawn)/Rebecca

Early 1667

Mount Faith Manor Plantation, Barbados

Morning arrives whether I have slept or not. I lie in my hammock, still, listening to the monkeys and birds, screeching and singing as they wake up. The fireworks that lit the sky throughout the night seemed not to have bothered the animals at all. Today is just another day; the sun rises no matter what has happened. MaNa's warm little body lies next to me. The sounds and lights frightened her, so she abandoned her hammock for mine. Now we are both hot and sweaty.

The English on the island have been celebrating the beginning of the new year for many days, culminating in the biggest parties last night. We do not celebrate here at Mount Faith Manor because our owners are religious Quakers; they do not believe in observing holidays created by man. There was no escaping the sounds of revelry taking place elsewhere in Bridgetown, though.

Compared to many slaves on the island, we have a fairly decent life; at least, that is what Elizabeth says. Master White is kinder than most plantation owners, from what I have heard and observed. He and his wife, Mistress Sarah, are teaching me to speak and read English, and I can even write a bit. They read their book called the Bible daily after the evening meal. The slaves are allowed and encouraged to attend on a rotating basis, to listen and observe as the family prays. They speak of their God and his son, Jesus. Their God is like our Great Hare. They believe he created the world. Their Jesus is different, maybe like our O'Ki'Us, overseeing the behavior of the people, but then again, I am not sure. It is confusing.

I hear the morning bell ringing and unstick myself from MaNa and leave the hammock. She rolls to the middle, unperturbed. I pull on an ivory linen skirt and top; then wrap my head in another piece of the same fabric. All the slaves across the island wear clothes made of the same coarse linen called osnaburg. It makes us easily identifiable, and it is supposedly the coolest material for working in the scorching sugar cane fields. We live in a little square hut that is made of cut stone with a dirt floor. It has a thatched roof and a wooden door with open windows on the three other sides that allow a breeze to blow through.

MaNa and I live in this one room cottage with two other women and a young boy of perhaps six years of age. They are African slaves. Three other PaTow'O'Mek women, including my mother, live at Mount Faith Manor plantation and Elizabeth is here, too. We were not allowed to share quarters and were split up when we arrived. My mother was assigned a hut with Elizabeth and other African slaves who had already been living here. Thankfully, MaNa and I were allowed to stay together.

We have started harvesting the sugar cane, and it is brutal work. The men are charged with cutting the tall stalks at the plant base and as the cane falls to the ground they continue to move through the fields, slashing with their oversized machetes. Then the women gather the plants and when our arms are full, we place the bundles upright in a cart that is hitched to a donkey or cow. We take turns walking with the cart to the windmill where we feed the stalks into a large apparatus that crushes the plants and the sweet juice flows out into troughs, ready to be cooked into sugar.

I stroke MaNa's head gently as she sleeps before joining the other slaves as we walk toward the crops. The children of the slaves play together while we are out in the fields or in the sugar-processing mill. It is too dangerous for the little ones to be around us while we work. As we walk, we greet one another with silent nods, acknowledging we have lived through the night and will face another workday together. There is an overseer who is also a slave, but he carries a gun and whip to keep the harvesting moving at a swift pace. If the sugar cane is not processed quickly after it is cut, it will rot and become worthless. We work for several hours and then take a break to eat breakfast. We have a banana or a baked sweet potato and a bowl of gruel; thankfully it is better tasting than what we had on the *Trinity*. We drink water that has lemon or lime juice squeezed into it; sometimes the water is sweetened with molasses. A house slave brings the food to us in the field, we eat, and then we go back to work.

"Watch out, Rebecca!" The overseer yells, but I keep unloading the cart and feeding the cane into the grinder. "Rebecca!" He yells again, and I remember my new name is Rebecca and realize he is talking to me. I look toward him.

He motions for me to tuck my blouse into my skirt, which had worked its way out and is dangling. Just last week, one of the men was accidentally pulled into the rollers when his shirt sleeve got entangled and trapped him as he fought to get the shirt off. His arm was badly mangled and then amputated to save his life. There is a machete that stays near the rollers to cut off hands or arms that get caught, thus preserving the life of the slave, minus the captive appendage. He is still in the plantation sick house, one of the outbuildings for slaves to recover from injury or sickness.

I secure my blouse as he has ordered and continue lifting and shoving the cane. Finally, the cart is empty, and I walk back toward the fields, leading the donkey by a rope, the cart bumping along behind us. My arms and back ache. I wish I could sit down and rest. My mind wanders back to the days of harvest in *TseNaCoMoCo*; it was so different as we laughed with each other and worked at a relaxed pace. I think about Xo. I wonder how she and WaBus are doing. They were both sold to another plantation on the terrible day we anchored in Barbados, and I have not seen or heard from them since.

* * *

CAPTAIN THOMAS HAD BEEN IN A LONG, heated discussion with a tall, bearded fellow. The man was wearing gray pants and vest, a long-sleeved white shirt, his head covered with a wide brimmed black hat. He seemed overdressed for the sweltering heat that was bearing down on all of us. As we tried to eavesdrop, the first mate gathered me and MaNa, my mother, Elizabeth and three other PaTow'O'Mek captives, removing us from the larger group.

Captain Thomas said to the man, "Here, take them. This more than repays you for the loss of the other three Africans. Moving slaves is always a risky business; you know that, Master White. Your brother knew it, too. There were no guarantees." His hand is behind his back, as usual, his fingers feeling the cat of nine tails beneath his jacket.

Master White, the gentleman in the black hat, did not raise his voice. His controlled demeanor while negotiating was in stark contrast to Captain Thomas's agitated rumblings.

"Good day to thee, Captain Thomas," Master White said and motioned for the seven of us to move toward the rope ladder and dinghy that bobbed in the water below.

My heart was breaking to leave behind Xo and WaBus. I looked back to my tribe members huddled on deck; we all feared for our fates but were helpless to change anything. I broke from the departing group and ran to Xo, clinging to her and she to me.

Through my tears I choked out the words, "*NihTe KihTe*', my heart your heart."

One of the crew immediately dragged me from her and I reached for WaBus, our fingers finding each other for a brief second, *"Nir PaXeNa'An Nes*, I will find you."

I tell her again, *"Nir PaXeNa'An Nes*, I will find you!"

My body felt as heavy as a fallen tree as the sailor pulled me toward the ladder. I joined the group of slaves who now belonged to Master Russell White, owner of Mount Faith Manor, a sugar plantation.

* * *

"Rebecca!"

I jolt back to reality and away from my memories by someone shouting my name. "Rebecca!"

It is the overseer again. He has left the mill and is now in the field. I look at my blouse, but it is tucked in, so I look at him with questioning eyes.

"Faster, faster—load the cane," he barks at me, sweeping his hand toward the fallen produce. He puts his hands on his gun for emphasis, making it clear that he is in charge and can order all of us according to his whim. His skin is very black in color, his clothing the white linen garb we all wear. The only difference is the gun he has strapped across his chest and the whip tucked into the waist of his pants. He does not help with the work. He clearly relishes his position of authority and calls out to the workers throughout the day, urging them to go faster.

We all suffer from cuts and bruises, from the cane or accidents with the carts running over our feet. Everyone who works in the boiling house has burns, either from spills or splatter as the cane juice is heated and purified, ladled from one huge pot to the next.

The cows and mules often revolt and bite us. Rats run from the fields, disturbed from their nests by the noisy action. Sometimes, the machete-wielding men kill the rats, which are then roasted and eaten when we return to our huts, exhausted and starving from harvesting. We often work through the night. These are very long days, longer than when we arrived and spent our time weeding the fields and harvesting the sustenance crops. At least then, we had some time to tend our own gardens but not now.

The slaves who were here before we arrived tell me this frantic pace is just until the harvest is over. The older woman who shares our hut has skin the color of antimony, the deep black dye we used to collect and trade in *TseNaCoMoCo*. Her name is Ruth.

She mumbles under her breath when we move in, "Eat or die, eat or die." It makes no sense until the pace picks up and there is hardly any time to eat.

At first, MaNa was afraid of her and hid behind me when she spoke. MaNa is won over when Ruth magically pulls a piece of sugar candy from her pocket and hands it to my little Butterfly.

Elizabeth quickly learns from the long-time slaves; she remembers some African words and everyone here knows some English. She has taken the PaTow'O'Mek women now enslaved with her at Mount Faith Manor under her wing, helping us with our gardens, telling us who to avoid. I know she misses Xo. She credits Xo with saving her life. Maybe that is why she tries to keep us alive now. She surprises me with her cunning, sneaking into our hut at night. We, the newly purchased slaves, are warned repeatedly, to be careful, that there is always death during the harvest.

The only time I smile is when I return to the shelter I share with MaNa, Ruth and the others. Master White has given my MaNa the English name Mary, but I still call her MaNa, my Butterfly, when we are alone. I don't want her to forget her real name or her people, the PaTow'O'Mek. I have promised every God I know, and those I do not know, that we will return to *TseNaCoMoCo*. We cannot live here with these Strangers for the rest of our lives. I want a better existence for MaNa. I have promised my mother I will do this no matter what it takes.

* * *

WHEN WE ARRIVED AT MOUNT FAITH MANOR, I begged to live in the same dwelling with my mother, but *Nek* was assigned to another hut, with none of our other tribal members. I was glad that at least Elizabeth was with her, a familiar face and an experienced slave. My mother was sent into the field to weed with all the others that first day. Master White allowed me to be with MaNa because she was hysterically crying, and he told the overseer I could stay behind and try to get her settled. It was an unexpected act of kindness after the atrocities we had lived and witnessed.

That evening when *Nek* was returning from the fields, MaNa and I ran out to meet and walk with her. She was having trouble speaking and I thought perhaps she was just overtired. I helped her to her hammock, and she closed her eyes. Elizabeth sat with her while I ran to get water and food. When I returned, one side of her face was slack and the eye on that side would not open. She tried to speak to me, but it was garbled.

"What, *Nek*? What are you saying?" I leaned in close to her mouth to listen. Her lips moved again, but no sounds came out.

"Please drink a sip of water," I said, holding the cup to her lips. The water just dripped from her lips onto her neck.

"*Nek*, don't go. Please stay with me and MaNa."

Elizabeth began a low-pitched chanting in her African tongue. She rose and walked slowly around us, still chanting. She didn't have to explain; I knew it was a prayer to her God, the prayer when death was near. Ruth slipped into the hut and joined Elizabeth in the ritual. If we had been in *TseNaCoMoCo*, there would have been others to witness and share in the passage. There was comfort in their presence at this sacred and sad time.

I sat beside my mother's hammock and held her hand, reminding her that she was loved and that she had lived a meaningful life. I spoke of her son, my brother A'KwiMex, and how happy we had been together in *TseNaCoMoCo*, living near the banks of the Potomac River.

"*Nek*, remember when A'KwiMex returned from *HusKaNaw* with the snake earring? How we all laughed, it was so unexpected. Remember how later I imitated him, putting a skinny green snake in my earlobe, too?"

Her eyes were closed, but I thought I saw her smile. I hummed and tried to sing the songs of our tribe, songs of mourning and transition. My words were barely audible; my throat was filled with grief.

"When Spirit speaks, we listen.

When Earth speaks, we listen.

It is so, it is so.

When Spirit calls, we follow.

When Earth calls, we follow.

It is so, it is so."

I had seen this before, when Spirit and Earth call. I knew she was dying. After so much loss, I was numb. My throat thickened and my heart felt heavy. The river of tears would come later. I thought about the voyage on the *Trinity* and how difficult it had been and how her hair had turned almost completely white.

Losing A'KwiMex had been too much to bear; she never really got over the massacre of all the men. I sat with her at the side of her hammock, holding her hand, with MaNa in my lap. She passed from this life with my daughter and me asleep beneath her hammock. Elizabeth and Ruth stopped their song and sat beside us. Elizabeth picked up a handful of dirt from the floor and lightly threw it into the air. Spirit.

In the morning, the overseer came with a cart, loaded her body and put her in the ground beyond the sugar cane, a place where all the slaves were buried. That was just our second day in Barbados.

* * *

Now I stand outside the wooden door of our stone dwelling before opening it. My heart is heavy with missing my mother, so I take a deep breath to lighten my being before greeting my daughter. She is usually playing outside when I return each evening and she always runs to meet me with a smile on her perfect face. There are other children standing around, but I do not see her. I am sure she is inside. I open the door slowly in case she is playing a hiding game with me and has chosen a spot behind the door. I want to humor her and play along.

"MaNa, where are you?" I whisper. As my eyes adjust to the dark space, I notice she is in my hammock. She looks to be asleep; again I am sure she is trying to amuse me by playing opossum.

"MaNa," I whisper. "I see you."

I walk to her and reach out to her sleeping body. As I touch her, I tremble in horror. She is burning up with fever. I now realize she has not left my hammock all day, and she is soiled with her own waste. I pick her up and cradle her in my arms.

"*MaTa*, no, my darling, you must not be sick, I cannot lose you, too."

I do not cry. I run out the door with her in my arms, racing as fast as I can to the slave sick house for help. When I get to the sick hut, there is no one to help, just the injured slaves trying to recover. I run toward Master White's large house, with its glass windows and stone floors. I keep going past the kitchen building and push my way through the back door into the main house and fall to my knees and find my voice.

"Help me, help MaNa, help my Mary," I plead, using her English name. The house slaves look horrified to see me intrude in this way. Field slaves are only allowed inside for prayer and never unannounced.

Two of them run to my sides and try to shuffle me out before the Master and Mistress are disturbed. I will not go without a fight.

But I do not have to fight. Mistress Sarah hears the commotion and follows the sound to me and my feverish daughter.

"What is happening?" She asks as she kneels and places her hand on MaNa's head. She immediately lifts MaNa out of my arms and moves briskly down the hall to a large room, calling for water and rags as she walks. She lays my daughter on a low bed they call a divan and begins to gently wipe her with the water.

"Bring the sugar wine," she instructs the house help. She pours a spoonful and places the liquid into MaNa's mouth. For the first time since I found her unconscious, she sputters, reacting to the medicine.

Mistress Sarah continues to care for MaNa by sponging her off to help break the fever. Master White has watched from his chair in the corner where he reads and occasionally asks a few questions. Twilight turns to dark night, and candles now illuminate the room.

"Wife," he says, clearing his throat. "It will be best to take the child to the sick house, and her mother can care for her there or another slave can attend to her."

Mistress Sarah hesitates before she answers. "I think not. She is too young for the sick house. I will tend to her here and see that she is properly cared for," she says as she looks first to her husband and then to me. "And her mother will stay here and help me."

"I do not think this is a good idea, Sarah. It sends the wrong message. We can't care for all the sick here in our house. We have a building specifically made to treat the sick and injured slaves."

"Russell, please. After all that has happened, surely thou will not turn thy back on this child," she says. The Whites have no living children. According to the other slaves, they had a son and daughter, both of whom died of fever before we arrived.

Master White looks defeated when reminded of their loss and says, "Sarah, we tried and did everything to no avail. I can't—." He stops mid-sentence.

He seems to change course and says, "The best thing we can do is to pray for the child and that her soul will go to heaven."

Master White and Mistress Sarah kneel beside the couch where MaNa is lying, still unresponsive. "Join us, Rebecca."

So I kneel beside them and listen. They take turns speaking to their God and sometimes they call on his son Jesus. Mistress Sarah prays that Mary will be healed, and Master White prays that her soul will go to heaven if she dies. I am moved by their words, but it is all so strange and unfamiliar.

I haven't looked to the sky for the Great Hare in a long time; our PaTow'O'Mek custom of bathing and then praying each morning is a distant memory now. After the praying, they retire to their chairs, and I remain seated on the floor by my daughter.

We sit in silence until Master White says to me, "Rebecca, the God we worship is for everyone. He is for thee, too. He cares for Mary. The God we love has the power to heal Mary. We just have to ask Him to do it."

These words make me feel uneasy and I do not understand them, but I do understand that Master White has just said his God can cure Mary and restore her life. Is this true? Can this possibly be true? But if so, why did Master White's children die? Surely, he and Mistress Sarah prayed for them. It does not make sense, but I nod. I want their God or Jesus to heal Mary, my MaNa. With this nod, he gets the book about God, the Bible, and he begins reading it to me.

I am overwhelmed with exhaustion from the day's work and the emotional toll that finding my ailing child has wrought, my eyes are beginning to close and my head dropping when MaNa opens her eyes and says, "I'm thirsty."

Master White leaps to his feet and says, "Praise be, Father God, we give Thee thanks!" He lifts his hands in the air and looks to the ceiling.

Mistress Sarah begins to cry and clasps my hand and then moves to MaNa, "Oh, Mary, thou art healed. Praise God!"

And then Master White says these words directly to me: "Because thou believed, Rebecca, God has healed Mary."

Xo
(Shining Moon)/Leah

EARLY 1667

SUGAR GROVE PLANTATION, BARBADOS

I am filled with rage, but it is masked as indifference. This monster will never know how I really feel.

Master Lewis does his "business," as he calls it, relentlessly bouncing his fat belly on top of me, making it difficult to breathe. He belches in my face. The sour smell of too much sugar wine mixed with oily meat and other poorly digested indulgences from the weeklong celebration wafts through my nostrils.

He laughs when I turn my head in disgust, but he follows the laugh with a vicious slap to the side of my head that makes my ear sting. It does, however, thrill him enough that he finishes and rolls off, panting.

I have never consented to these forced couplings. He has come to my hut for this business at least twenty times since we were sold off the slave ship *Trinity*. While he stands and pulls up his breeches, I imagine what it would be like to cut his throat, the way Eightyseven killed the sailors when we tried to mutiny. She did it so expertly, I have often wondered if she had killed before. But my thoughts return to this beast standing in front me: Would he whimper with fright or scream in terror? Could he overpower me and kill me even as he bled out? I do not know the answers to these questions.

As he opens the door to leave, he looks back at me and says, "Happy New Year, Leah."

I take a deep breath and sit up, gathering my clothes to dress and prepare to head for the fields to help with the sugar cane harvest. I usually wash the laundry for Master and Mistress Lewis, their children and the body slaves who work in the main house, but I have been told to go to the field today and help with the harvest. As I open the door of my hut, WaBus and I almost collide. We hug and rub noses. When we were bought by Master Lewis to be his slaves, WaBus was taken from me to the main house to help with the three young Lewis children. She resides in a small room near the back of the house with the other house slaves, where they sleep on blankets on the floor. She is to be available at all hours should the children or Master and Mistress Lewis need assistance with anything during the night.

"Is everything all right, WaBuses?" I ask, addressing her by a term of endearment that means, "my little bunny." I have warned her to stay away from Master Lewis, to avoid being alone with him, no matter what. His reputation as a lecher is much discussed among the slaves, and Mistress Lewis abhors his proclivities, in turn flogging the recipients of his advances. I hear that he forces himself upon slave girls who have not yet experienced first blood, and I am determined that he will not do his business with WaBus.

"Yes, everything is fine, but Mistress Lewis wants you to come to the house instead of the field, as there is much washing to be done after the party last night," she says.

I am perplexed at this sudden change in plans, but I do as I am ordered and walk with my daughter in the direction of the large house. It is two stories tall, made of stone with a slate roof. I have not seen all the rooms, but WaBus says they are magnificent, with feather mattresses and pillows on top of polished wooden frames for sleeping, each bed with its own linen sheets and blankets. If the sleeping linens need to be changed, the housemaids

strip the beds and bring them to me along with clothing and undergarments for washing.

The washing area is a small stone cottage off the main house,
near the cistern, which collects rainwater that is used for bathing
and washing. The cottage has three rooms, the laundry washing
room, a room with a tub for bathing and a room that serves as the
latrine. The latrine has a wooden platform with holes cut in the
top for sitting. The waste goes into deep holes that have been dug
beneath. The slaves are not allowed to use the cottage latrine; it is
just for the plantation family and guests. We do our toileting in
a similar but more primitive version that is built behind the slave
huts, near the cane fields.

I go to the washing room to see if the dirty items are there yet.
A pile of bloody rags waits for me, but nothing else. During the
monthly bleeding, the English do not have a practice of seclusion
with other women as the PaTow'O'Mek did when we went to the
Mesk YiHaKan, the Blood House, for a time of rest and companionship. The slaves are not allowed to rest or isolate during their
monthly bleeding, either. Mistress Lewis "takes to her bed" during
that time; she calls it her "monthly sickness." To protect her clothes
from the blood, she folds fabric and fashions the pieces much like
a loin cloth, secured around her waist with another strip of cotton.
Her personal slave collects the soiled, blood-soaked rags, and they
will be washed and prepared for reuse the following month. The
slaves must also use cotton or linen rags during monthly shedding;
the rags are also washed and reused. At first it seemed disgusting
to wash the bloody rags, but I am used to it now.

I get a bucket and fill it from the cistern and go back into the
building to soak and scrub the blood out of the fabric. I fill the tub
from the bucket and add the bloody rags, agitating them with a
stick to loosen the dried blood. I am mindlessly stirring, watching
the blood clots loosen and float when I am struck from behind
with a whip. I whirl around with the washing stick raised to protect

myself and see that it is Mistress Lewis. Her face is red and twisted in anger and she raises the whip to flog me again, but I hold up the stick with both hands.

"How dare you raise your hands against me! Put down that stick immediately!" Mistress Lewis, the lady of the house, continues, "You ungrateful savage, constantly seducing Master Lewis. I know he came to you this morning to do his business. Take off your blouse and put your hands on the wall, right now!"

I have been verbally chastised and threatened by Mistress Lewis, but not physically assaulted by her until today. She is enraged that her husband has intimate relations with the slave women at Sugar Grove Plantation. He has fathered several slave children in addition to the three Mistress Lewis has borne him.

I slowly take off my shirt and let it fall from my shoulders; it is tucked into my skirt. She makes a small gasp when she sees my back. I guess she had forgotten about, or never noticed my flower tattoos and the scars from the beating on the *Trinity*. She recovers and flogs me, counting to twenty as she strikes. I close my eyes and will myself not to flinch, but I cannot help it. Each blow stings and cuts. I feel the blood begin to flow. I imagine it is the flowers on my back crying, the tears made of blood. My back weeps for all that was: for my lost son, for my husband, my mother. There is no end to the loss and my back carries all of it. The blows finally cease.

Mistress Lewis is out of breath but manages to say as she straightens her skirt, "One stripe for every time you whored with my husband."

I remain with my hands on the wall, facing away from her and she leaves.

This place, this island is barbaric. They call us savages, but the English are the real barbarians. The way it started was inhumane, and it has continued to be so. I think back to that awful day, just one among many terrible days, but it stands apart from the rest because it was the first day on the island.

* * *

WE WERE ALL ON THE LOWER DECK of the *Trinity* when a man with a black hat took Ah'SaWei, her mother, MaNa, Elizabeth and three other tribe members off the ship. We watched the negotiations, not knowing what was happening, and then everything moved so quickly. When Ah'SaWei ran to me, my heart was bursting to think I would never see her again.

I still hear her voice and replay the scene over and over in my mind, "*NihTe KihTe*', my heart, your heart."

It comforts me and simultaneously breaks me every time I remember that moment. As I watched her leave, another small boat was approaching the *Trinity*, this one filled with eight English men, each holding lengths of rope, coiled into bundles. When they boarded, they conferred with Captain Thomas. I heard most of their conversation and understood that the rest of us would be sold by a scramble. But what is a scramble, I wondered.

The men walked around the group of PaTow'O'Mek captives, sizing us up, evaluating our worth. We stood there, shorn and oiled, naked except for our loincloths. At some point Captain Thomas initiated the so-called scramble. The men descended upon us, grabbing us by the wrists or waists, wrapping the ropes tightly around whatever part they grabbed and then continuing to add another captive to the chain. It was a riot of screams, slapping, hitting, pinching; no behavior was off limits.

Once we were all bound and held by our buyers, there was quiet. I had fiercely held onto WaBus, so when I was caught, she was caught with me. Some of the other mothers were separated from their children, and once we understood what was happening, how we were being sold, it was heartbreaking. There was a frantic attempt to reconfigure the groupings, but our new owners did not allow any changes. They gave their gold pieces to Captain Thomas and the sale was complete. Group by group, we rowed to shore to begin our new lives on Barbados island.

WaBus and I were now the property of Master James Lewis, owner of the Sugar Grove Plantation, just outside of Bridgetown. From the first moment I saw him, I felt his spirit was nefarious. He was of medium height compared to the other English men I had seen but, unlike most, his stomach was exceedingly fat. His face was reddish in color and his hair yellow, looking somewhat like straw. He carried a flask in his outer coat pocket and drank from it frequently, making a smacking sound with his lips after each draw. When we got to the dock, he whistled using his fingers, and a carriage with a cart attached appeared, pulled by two horses. The driver was a thin black man, taller than Master Lewis by a foot, wearing white pants and shirt. The driver had no shoes.

Master Lewis ordered us to get into the cart. His purchases were ten of the PaTow'O'Mek captives: six women, three boys and one girl, that girl being my daughter, WaBus. He sat up front with the driver, and the Big Dogs began to move. It was a bumpy ride in the back of the four-wheeled cart and we fell into one another as we were packed so close together. I hardly noticed the jostling, as my eyes were mesmerized by all that I was seeing. There were so many people in the streets. It was loud with their voices talking and yelling to one another. They were English mostly, but other people as well. There were pale men with long dark beards, dressed all in black. There were black people, all of them dressed in light-colored clothing. The black women often had big baskets balanced on their heads as they walked along. The containers were filled with many different kinds of produce. I recognized corn, bananas and yams.

The smell at the dock was of salt water, urine and sweat emanating from unwashed, working bodies, but as we moved away from the bustling city, the smell of the earth and rain became more prominent, mixed with the fragrant bouquet of the flowers that blossomed everywhere. I did not realize at the time that the sweet scent of the frangipani trees, hibiscus bushes and bougainvillea plants would be an ever-present background as I experienced my new life.

When we arrived at Sugar Grove Plantation, I was shocked about the size; it appeared as big as our village in *TseNaCoMoCo*, or even bigger. We turned onto a dirt road that had blooming cherry trees flanking both sides. At last, a huge dwelling appeared, a house on top of a house, or so it seemed! The horses drew the cart around the big structure, and from there you could see the smaller cooking house and several other outbuildings.

Master Lewis called out the names of them as we were passing.

"There is the bathing and washing house, there you see the barn, this is the pasture." Beyond that, a tall conical structure with four wings, similar to the sails on the *Trinity*.

"That's the mill, there you see the boiling house, this is the sick house—"

It was so much to take in and made more difficult by our limited understanding of English. I clutched WaBus's hand; her eyes were as wide as an owl's. Beyond the garden that was growing corn, beans and other foods I had never seen before, we at last saw our living quarters. The huts were small in comparison to the main house, with thatched coverings for the roof instead of slate. We stopped here and the driver went into one of the huts and returned with an armful of clothing. He distributed blouses and skirts for the women, breeches and blouses for the boys and WaBus was given a tunic of sorts. We got back in the cart, did a big loop, and returned to the large house. A woman and three children were standing outside, awaiting our arrival.

Master Lewis stepped off the carriage and motioned for the new possessions to get out of the cart and line up.

"Madam, here are the new slaves. Children, these are the new slaves," announced Master Lewis to his wife.

Mistress Lewis said brusquely, "I'll take her," pointing to WaBus. "What's her name?"

My smart daughter understood the question and answered, "WaBus."

Mistress Lewis chuckled but the tone was unfriendly. "No, I was not asking you. Do not speak unless you are addressed. And no, that will not do. We shall call you Anne."

"Come along, Anne, you will help with the children."

I felt my heart start to pound, I was not sure what was happening, so I stepped out of the line toward Anne, my WaBus.

"Get back right now!" Master Lewis walked toward me and pushed me back into the line. "We are not finished."

He turned to the driver, "Samuel, get the book so I can record the names."

After everything was said and done, I was renamed Leah. I was to be trained as a house slave to do the washing, but I would live in the huts with the field slaves. Anne, as a house slave to the children, would sleep in the main house. I vowed at that moment, and over and over again, to get out of Barbados as soon as possible, by whatever means necessary. I thought of my stolen baby son. I would never forget him; I would return and claim him. I would not stay here and have my daughter live in bondage to these people.

* * *

As I put my blouse on after the beating, I tell myself once again that this is temporary; WaBus and I will not stay here forever. There are stories of slaves who have escaped the plantations here in Barbados. Some live in the jungle for many moons and then are recaptured. Some escape to nearby islands and are never heard from again. Sometimes, a slave will run to another plantation and hide with the help of those slaves. That happens when families are separated and are desperate to see their spouses, parents, or children.

I asked the slaves who live here at Sugar Grove Plantation about the other PaTow'O'Mek slaves and was told our members are living all over the island. I ask specifically about Ah'SaWei and MaNa, but no one really knows. We do know a Quaker man bought her, and I am told there are quite a few Quaker plantations scattered throughout the parishes of Barbados. I am told the Quakers have a reputation for treating their slaves well and even teaching them to read and write English, and I hope that is true for Ah'SaWei.

My WaBus is learning English in spite of being forbidden to study. She listens as the Lewis children are taught and when WaBus is alone with the children, the oldest girl, Caroline, reads to her and teaches her the letters. I practice making letters with a stick in the dirt behind my quarters. I do not want to forget what Elizabeth taught me. I know I will need to read in order to escape.

I finish washing the monthly blood rags, rinse them, squeeze out the excess water and lay them out to dry in the sun on some nearby shrubs. If it does not rain, they will dry quickly. While the rain interferes with drying the washed laundry, it is such a welcome gift from nature. The rain here is warm and soft, even when it pours from the sky. It is refreshing, and afterwards the world smells clean and loamy. The smell reminds me of *CaHatTaYough*, early summer in *TseNaCoMoCo*, when we would till the earth and plant corn, squash and beans. There are just two seasons here, dry and hot, or rainy and hot. Even when it is the dry time, there is still rain, just not as much. There are always seeds to be planted, always fruits and vegetables to be harvested. The rhythm of life is completely different from my life with my tribe along the Potomac River.

There is a sameness here, and I miss the changing colors and falling of the leaves that we had during the Time for Gathering Nuts. I miss the white snow and the cold that came in *PoPaNaw*, winter.

But most of all, I miss my baby. I pray to the Great Hare and O'Ki'Us that my Strong Son is safe and cared for wherever he is. The kidnapping of our tribal children is not unheard of; it had happened even before our tribe was massacred. And it had happened to other tribes in *TseNaCoMoCo*. It had happened to my own brother. We knew of children who grew up with Strangers' families and then came back to their tribes when they were adults, and often reported that they had been treated kindly. I hope he is being treated well, but no matter. I will see Strong Son again. I will hold him in my arms once more.

Ah'SaWei

(Golden Fawn)/Rebecca

Spring, 1668

Mount Faith Manor, Barbados

O ur lives changed completely after MaNa was healed of her fever. Mistress Sarah wanted to keep a close eye on her as she recovered. MaNa, who was now called Mary, moved into one of the bedrooms that had been empty since both of the Whites' children died of fever. I was elevated from being a field slave to the better station of house slave. And because of that, I was moved from my hut near the cane fields to a small room at the back of the main house that I shared with Lucy, another house slave. Mary's care was taken over by Mistress Sarah while I learned how to wash laundry and began to cook in the English way, assisting the African cook, Betty.

At the next Sunday meeting of the Friends, as Master White called the believers of his religion, the Whites invited Mary and me to attend and sit with them, instead of with the other slaves. The men sat on one side of the room, the women together opposite the men so at this meeting, MaNa and I were sitting beside Mistress Sarah. I had been in attendance previously, curiously watching as the participants sat quietly, often with their eyes closed, praying silently. Master White explained to me that they were waiting for God to inspire them to speak. It could take quite a while for the words to come and the quiet made me sleepy, startling to wakefulness when the message was finally spoken. At this meeting, however, Master White could hardly contain himself, and within minutes of the silence commencing, he rose to his feet with a word.

"I rise to speak with thee, my fellow believers, God has worked a miracle at Mount Faith Manor in recent days. One of our newest slaves, Rebecca," he paused and looked at me, "has been convinced to become a believer in Christ Jesus."

I could feel myself flush with the attention caused by the announcement as the other congregants turned to look at me.

He continued, "Rebecca's young daughter, Mary, became very ill with fever sickness and Sarah and I feared she would die, just as our two precious children had succumbed. As we thus prayed for the child to recover or for her soul to be received by our Lord, Rebecca prayed with us."

Mistress Sarah put her arms protectively around Mary but looked at me and smiled.

"As thee can see, Mary was healed and is with us today, praise be to God." With that emotional disclosure, he sat down, trembling.

A quiet murmuring rippled through the group and again silence. Mary fell asleep, her head resting on Mistress Sarah, who was caressing my daughter's hair. I was filled with conflicting emotions. I was grateful my cherished MaNa was alive, but in that moment, I wished she was asleep on my shoulder and that I could be the one stroking her head. They were treating us well—but we were still slaves. I did want to believe in the God and the Jesus of the Friends, but I still found myself looking to the sky for the Great Hare.

As Mary was so young, she quickly learned the Bible stories that Mistress Sarah read to her. My daughter spoke easily of Jesus. As the moons came and went, Mary could recite Bible verses by memory, much to the delight of Master and Mistress White. Mistress Sarah began to dress MaNa in the left-behind clothes of her deceased daughter. MaNa no longer wore the white linen that marked the rest of us as slaves. Now she wore blue or brown cotton dresses with white collars. The other slaves at Mount Faith Manor noticed the change and occasionally remarked on this development. Elizabeth seemed especially irritated that MaNa and I had been pulled from the field to the house to work. I didn't know how to respond to what felt like a criticism from Elizabeth; her friendship meant a lot to me as we had experienced so much on the *Trinity* and then the death of my mother. I had no control over these developments with MaNa or myself.

I went to the slave huts near the sugar cane fields only on Fridays now, to help deliver the weekly rations. The field slaves were supplied breakfast and lunch as they worked but Master White himself distributed food rations for dinners on Friday evenings, for the slaves to prepare as they wished during the week. All of us as slaves also had our own gardens where we grew the fruits and vegetables native to Barbados. We had okra, mango and yams that had been seeded from Africa. The weekly allotments from Master White were meager, so the gardens were a necessity to keep from starving. The rations usually included salted fish, sweet potatoes and corn. The salted fish were similar to the dried fish we preserved in our tribe, except in Barbados they were cured using salt.

Betty, the cook, taught me to make a tasty stew with pounded corn that was boiled with the saltfish and chilies from the garden, thickened with cassava flour. This stew was a filling staple of the field slaves. Occasionally, the snouts, feet and ears of pigs would be given as a part of the ration. The Africans made a soup they called *souse* from these leftover parts by boiling the meat to tenderize it and then marinating it in a mixture of lime juice, peppers, onions, cucumbers and garlic.

Once I became a house slave, my diet had more variety and was of better quality. I ate leftovers from the meals prepared for the Whites. They had meat at least once a day, pork mostly, but chicken, too. Gravies were made with the pork and chicken dishes. There was an abundance of fleshy fish that were roasted and served with sauce made from papaya. There were also sweet puddings and breads, all new to me, but delicious.

One Friday night, Elizabeth helped me distribute the rations. "Where's your Mary?"

"She's at the big house with Mistress Sarah." It was an odd question. Of course, Mary was at the main house.

"I seen her dressed like an English girl, not a slave," mused Elizabeth.

"Yes, the dresses belonged to the Whites' daughter, the little one who died, and Miss Sarah said she didn't want to waste them."

"Hmmm." Elizabeth harumphed and then, "You better watch out."

"What do you mean, watch out?"

"What I said, you better watch out," repeated Elizabeth and she walked away.

I knew there was resentment between the house slaves and the field slaves. The field slaves believed the house slaves were treated better, and perhaps they were right. Certainly the food was an improvement. The sleeping quarters were more comfortable, too, but these things were balanced out by what we missed. We lost the camaraderie that existed in the slave quarters when the slaves had time together late in the evenings, or on the Sundays off when it was not harvesting season. But the reality was that none of us had any say in our station in life or our assigned jobs.

I turned to run and catch up with Elizabeth, grabbing her arm as she tried to ignore me. "What can I do, Elizabeth? There is nothing I can do! What can I do?"

She had no answer, but her words troubled me.

Elizabeth knew I was right, there was nothing I could do short of escaping the island and taking MaNa with me.

Again, but this time with softness in her voice, she said, "Better be careful, better watch out."

* * *

WHILE I HAD NEVER SEEN MASTER WHITE flog or physically punish any of his slaves, if he was dissatisfied, the overseer acted as his proxy and did not hesitate to whip the offender using a long leather strap attached to a wooden handle. That whip and the presence of the thunder stick kept us in line, prevented us from having the freedom we longed to have.

Over the next months, I was able to improve my English speaking, reading, and writing skills. I also learned how to prepare the traditional foods of England and Barbados from the bounty that grew in the garden. While I was familiar with corn, green beans and squash, there were so many new foods to learn about. Here we had mango, papaya, melons, figs and more. I learned how to cook chicken and pig. Sometimes we slowly smoked thin slices of meat, threaded on green wood skewers, for hours over a low fire. I learned to make many new types of soup and stew.

The cook, Betty, introduced the White family to an African stew that used okra, crab and coconut that was called *calalu*. It was delicious and different from the soups we made in *TseNaCoMoCo*. She taught me about the spices of the island, like ginger and pepperroot. She was friendly and enjoyed having extra help in the kitchen. She wanted to know all about the foods we ate in our tribe. Telling her about our ground corn bread filled with walnuts or wild strawberries brought fond memories of home to my mind. I found myself rambling on and on about roasted eel and our dried fish.

She delighted in hearing about our diet. If I stopped talking, she said, "More, girl. Tell me more."

My previous experience with drying and grinding of corn and tuckahoe was helpful, and I quickly acclimated to cooking with the new ingredients. As I became more comfortable and trusted in the kitchen, Betty let me introduce the family to fried corn pone cakes, which they improved upon by dipping in molasses. We did not have sugar in our tribe in *TseNaCoMoCo*. The only sweet ingredient we knew of was honey that we took from wild beehives, which we usually ate straight from the waxy comb. We had not always had honey; it was new to us, as the Strangers had brought honeybees from their homeland. The only other sweet things we had were fruits like wild strawberries and blackberries or the drop of nectar we would taste from the white blooms on vines that grew in the forest.

MaNa became very fond of the custards I learned to make with cream and sugar, topping the sweet treat with fresh fruit. We used sugar liberally in many dishes, but mostly to make fruit jams, pies and to flavor drinks. Betty would spend much time carefully stirring a pot of boiling sugar over the flames before pouring it out and cutting it into small pieces of hard candy. She had perfected the art of candy-making. If it boiled too long, the sugar would harden too quickly and could not be cut into squares. If that happened, she broke it into pieces with a mallet. If it was undercooked, the end product was a sticky mess. No matter how it turned out: too sticky, too hard or perfect, it was tasty and eaten up without complaint.

The Whites also owned a small trading business in the city of Bridgetown. I learned about imported preserved English foods such as anchovies, and pickled oysters; olives and olive oil from Spain, delicacies that were sold in the shop on Tudor Street. Master White sent molasses and sugar to England and in return brought these traditional British foods to Barbados. The Whites' shop also sold or traded candles, pewter and china plates, glassware, and ceramic bowls for use in the kitchen. The store had a large section of fabric for sewing clothing. While the Quakers wore only simple garments made of cotton or finer linen than that of the slaves, Master Lewis sold silks and brocades, as there was a high demand for luxury fabrics from the wealthy planter class on the island. Itinerant tailors and seamstresses traveled from plantation to plantation for days at a time, sewing for families.

A slave named Isaac at Mount Faith Manor drove Master White into the city several times a week for the buying or selling of merchandise at the shop. In addition to driving the carriage, Isaac oversaw the team of Big Dogs that pulled the carriage or the cart. Isaac was mild-mannered and gentle with the animals and used his whip sparingly. More than once, I found him in the barn, hand feeding them pieces of yellow apple, or brushing their coats and speaking quietly to them.

Isaac was tall and thin. His posture made him appear regal. I could imagine him as a Chief of his tribe in Africa, but he never mentioned such a thing to me. He was amiable, smiling, and he always addressed me formally as Miss Rebecca. Since becoming a house slave, I saw him often, being sent to the barn to find him and deliver messages about chores or going to town or another plantation. I started to feel we were becoming friends.

I had been sent to the barn one morning to tell Isaac that Master White was not feeling well and planned to stay at the plantation but that he wanted Isaac to go into Bridgetown without him, taking a supply order that needed immediate attention.

I knocked at the opening to the barn to announce my arrival.

"Morning, Miss Rebecca. What's you needing today?" Isaac asked.

"Master White is unwell, but he wants you to go on to the shop in town without him. He said to get the Big Dogs, I mean, horses, ready to go."

Isaac smiles when I use the wrong word but there is kindness in his expression, we are all learning new languages.

"Aye, Miss Rebecca—Master White has to give me the paper so I can go alone. I'll get the horses ready, and you get the paper?"

As I walked to the house, I wondered what it would be like to go into town and see the store. I had heard so much about the textiles, kitchen supplies and preserved foods, and had seen many of the items at Mount Faith Manor, but I had never been to the store. I had also heard Tudor Street referred to when various visitors to Mount Faith Manor discussed importing and exporting. Tudor Street was also called Quaker Street because so many of the Friends owned businesses or lived there. I was intrigued and wanted to see it with my own eyes. I needed to see more of this island, to find a way to return to my homeland with my MaNa.

I found Master White sitting at his desk preparing the paper that would allow Isaac to be on the road to Bridgetown by himself.

"Rebecca, is Isaac here yet?"

"He will be here shortly, Master White."

As I stood there, Mistress Sarah came into the room holding MaNa's hand. "Russell, will you add three yards of pale gray batiste to the list? I want to have a new dress made for Mary. She is outgrowing all the dresses we had left after—" Her voice drifted off.

"Mother," Mary said, addressing Mistress Sarah. Her English was almost flawless. "May I have a blue dress instead of gray? Blue is my favorite color!"

My heart pounded within my chest to hear my daughter call another woman "Mother," even if it was in English. A flood of emotions washed over me. When had this happened?

Mistress Sarah sensed my discomfort, but said, "But of course, my darling Mary, you may have a new blue dress. Russell, make that three yards of light blue batiste, please," she said as she smiled at Mary. "Perhaps Rebecca should ride into Bridgetown with Isaac, to keep him company. That way, Mary can read to you while you rest. She is learning so much, I want you to see how very smart she is becoming."

In the span of minutes, my thoughts turned upside down. I had just been contemplating a way to finagle myself into town with Isaac. Now, witnessing the growing bond between the Whites and MaNa, all I wanted in this moment was to stay at the plantation, and remind Mary that her real name was MaNa and that she was a PaTow'O'Mek girl and that I was her only true mother.

Before I could protest, even though I had no grounds upon which to protest, as my life was not my own, Master White said, "That is an excellent idea. I had been pondering the idea myself. Rebecca has learned so much, it occurred to me that she could go into town and help with the shop herself."

He turned to me, "Rebecca, I'll add your name to the document, and thou may accompany Isaac."

All I could do was answer, "Aye, sir." I left the room with the papers in hand. I found my wide-brimmed hat to protect me from the omnipresent sun and stepped outside to meet Isaac.

We rode in silence. I was confused about my feelings, but not knowing Isaac well enough, I did not want to confide in him. He was clearly a trusted slave. I had to be careful not to show my dismay to someone who might betray me.

After a while, Isaac pointed out trees along the road and said, "See them trees? See them long roots hanging down? They're called 'bearded fig trees.' The island is named after them. Barbados means 'bearded ones.' When the first explorers found these islands, they named it after the trees that seemed to be growing beards."

All I could think of to say was, "Aye." I could tell he was trying to be friendly, and I wanted to reciprocate, but my mind was back at the plantation, wondering what MaNa was doing with Mistress Sarah.

As we approached Bridgetown, more carriages and carts appeared. It seemed like utter chaos with the streets and noises, vendors selling their wares.

Isaac sensed my anxiety. "Don't worry, Miss Rebecca, I'll show you everything. Once you come to town a few times, it's not confusing at all."

He was explaining where we were, but the names were not registering with me. Suddenly at the intersection of two larger streets, there was a terrible sight and smell. It was a large cage filled with Africans, men and women. It was horrifying to see them crowded together. Some curled on the ground, some yelling at passersby and some with tears streaming from their eyes. Some were naked, some with just loincloths.

"What's that?"

"That be 'the cage,' the place where runaways are stored until their owners come and retrieve them."

A shudder ran through me, seeing the conditions I would endure if I attempted to escape and failed. I could not bear the thought of MaNa being imprisoned in the cage.

We turned onto Tudor Street, and Isaac brought the carriage to a stop. He tied the horses to a post and helped me step off. He pointed out a lush garden and said it was where some of the Quaker Friends were buried. Beyond the Quaker burial garden was a large building that Isaac described as a synagogue, a place of worship but not for Quakers. There was so much to see and learn, it was overwhelming.

Inside the shop was a bustle of activity. The shopkeeper greeted Isaac and in turn, Isaac introduced me. The shopkeeper and his slaves bundled and weighed merchandise and took it to load on the waiting carts. The walls were lined with goods, arranged in sections with food in one place, fabrics rolled in big bolts somewhere else, kitchen wares in another spot. It was intriguing. I mostly just watched in awe as merchants and people bartered and decided on their purchases. I do not know how long we were there, but it was early evening as we loaded the cart and started back to Mount Faith Manor.

"I want to show you something, Miss Rebecca," Isaac said. We went past the Quaker burial ground to the front of the synagogue. "Just look at this building, aye, it's something."

It really was unique and, once again, unlike anything I had seen before. It was made of large white stones that had been cut to the same rectangular shape. It was tall, like two or three houses on top of each other. But the feature that made it most different was the huge arched windows at the top. Similarly, the roof was rounded above each window. It was different from the surrounding buildings, whose roofs and windows were all angled. The men going into the building were different, too. All dressed in black, they had long beards. They wore tall black hats.

Isaac said, "They just believe in God, the same God of Master White, but not his son Jesus."

Perplexed, I asked, "Do you mean O'Ki'Us?"

"What?" Isaac's brow was furrowed.

We stared at one another quizzically and then started laughing, recognizing our experiences were so different. The African deities he knew were unlike my Great Hare and O'Ki'Us and that the God of the synagogue and the Jesus of the Quakers was different as well.

Dusk was falling as we returned to Mount Faith Manor. We rode the rest of the way in easy silence, listening to the evening sounds of the Barbados jungle. The cicadas were chirping loudly, which eerily sounded like screaming. I was sure now; I had a new friend in Isaac.

Xo
(Shining Moon)/Leah

I lie curled in my hammock in the hut that is my refuge but also my prison. Today, it is a sanctuary as I left the fields clutching my stomach. So many slaves get sick, no one pays any attention to my pain. They have seen this distress many times. I have lived here for more than twenty-four full moons, and fifteen slaves have died. WaBus and I are the only PaTow'O'Mek slaves still alive at Sugar Grove Plantation. All the others are dead, even the boys.

We have heard that most of our tribal members sold to other plantations are dead as well. I wonder if Ah'SaWei and MaNa are among the fatalities. No one knows. We PaTow'O'Mek are a strong, proud people and we are used to physical work, but our bodies are not familiar with the constant exertion required to cultivate and harvest sugar cane in the broiling sun, with minimal food or rest. I am not surprised to learn so many have perished. I have very little happiness living here as a slave, and the things I enjoyed with my tribe in *TseNaCoMoCo* are just memories now.

Another wave of cramping grips me, and I breathe with intention, in through my nose, out through pursed lips to control the pain. I remember my other labors and the anticipation of bringing new life into the world. My mother was my midwife when WaBus was born. Even though WaBus was my first baby, her arrival was straightforward, and she was strong, crying so powerfully, she announced her presence to the tribe! She nursed ravenously and grew fat and healthy.

When I became pregnant again, I thought it would be the same but the boy I delivered came too soon and never drew breath. His perfect little body fit into my two cupped hands. I examined his toes and fingers; he looked peaceful and at rest. And then, it happened again, another tiny son who came too early, even though I had been drinking the medicinal tea we used to maintain pregnancy to full term.

I thought the child I was carrying when my husband, Ninj A'PaTa, was killed would suffer the same fate, but O'Ki'Us heard my prayers and my third son was born full of life, looking just like his father. Even though my mother was very sick at the time of his birth, she insisted on being with me. WaBus was there, too. My mother told her how to make a mound of leaves and what items to gather for cutting and tying off the cord. After he was born, all four of us were wrapped together in a tanned hide, smiling and watching the sun set. He nursed and cooed; my mother hummed a song of thanksgiving. The memory of his birth is one of my happiest, especially because it was shared with my daughter and mother.

I had waited to name that baby boy, hoping if his name was not known, death could not find him. His secret name was ToWawh Nu'KwiSus, Strong Son. Our PaTow'O'Mek tradition was to give a secret name, known only to the immediate family. I alone whispered "ToWawh Nu'KwiSus" into his newborn ears. He had not received his public name when he was stolen from my arms on the march from our village to the slave ship *Trinity*. When I think about him now, I realize that he would no longer be a baby. He would have teeth. He would be walking and beginning to talk.

I wonder if his eyes are still light, or if the color changed as he grew. I realize he would have another name by now, and I wonder what it might be. I long to hold him in my arms again and whisper his birth name and tell him the stories of our tribe and of his brave father.

The next contraction is stronger, so I leave the hammock and kneel in the corner, feeling the urge to push. The tiny thing plops onto the ground, still encased in its sac of water. It was dead, of course, I knew it would be. I had missed three bleeding moons. I knew the baby belonged to Master Lewis, and I did not want to add another child to the brood he had already fathered on the plantation. Mistress Lewis is also with child now, as are two other slaves, made pregnant with his seed. His children from the slaves are mistreated by his wife. I knew I would kill her if she touched a child of mine. So I drank the tea made from the cotton root bark, which was used to induce contractions and end pregnancy. It was a well-known remedy practiced on the island due to the constant raping of slaves by their masters.

As I pick up the translucent sac that held the tiny baby, it bursts and the water drips between my fingers into the dirt. I can see it is a girl, no bigger than the palm of my hand. I know I have saved her from a life of pain. I have prevented her from suffering beatings and molestation. With a stick, I dig a hole in the dirt floor, right there in the corner of my hut, and bury the fifth child I had borne. I am bleeding quite a bit and still cramping, so I put a folded rag in place between my legs and lie down on the dirt floor beside the fresh grave. I close my eyes.

I am back in TseNaCoMoCo, standing on the banks of the Potomac River, with WaBus by my side. I see what looks like a large bird's nest, an eagle's nest, floating in the water. It sounds like there is a crying animal in the nest, so I begin to run into the water to see what it is and retrieve it. The water begins to churn, and a sudden squall appears, blowing the nest away from my reach. I can see into the structure that the crying is coming from a baby, and I recognize that it is ToWawh Nu'KwiSus.

My heart leaps within my chest, "My son is alive!" When I reach into the nest to grab him, I realize he is lying on three crushed eggs and the little eaglets are rotting beneath him. The putrid smell of death fills my nose as I lift him. I turn to show WaBus that her brother is saved, but she is no longer on the bank. She has somehow been carried down the river and is out of my reach. I try to run to her through the water while holding my son and she disappears under the waves.

An anguished cry from my own lips awakens me, my heart pounding with terror, and I realize it was just a dream, a nightmare. It is dusk and I remember I am in Barbados, a slave lying on an earthen floor, sweating with fever and bleeding from having given birth. I massage my belly to help stop the flow of blood and my efforts are successful. I drink some water from the clay jar we keep in our dwelling and walk to the door. As I look out, I think about my dream. What did it mean? I wish I could talk to my mother about it. She was very wise about such things. As I am thinking about her, I begin to understand the meaning of the dream. There is no doubt in my mind: My son is alive, *and* my daughter is in danger. I have to take care of them both, but how? I have to get WaBus off this plantation; I have to get back to my son, but how?

Over the coming days, I am consumed to the point of distraction trying to formulate an escape plan. I have been off the property just a handful of times since we arrived. I have been to Bridgetown to stand in the alley behind the Anglican church that the Lewises occasionally attend. Slaves are not allowed into the church building, but we are permitted to stand outside behind the building. Some of the slaves shout, "Amen" in response to the message. I do not want to hear about a God that allows men to beat, maim and abuse other people.

I use the time to observe the streets, walking to see if I can see the flying boats that brought us here. I get to a canal of sorts, there is water, but I can see land on the other side. Maybe it is like the Potomac River and opens into the bay and then the ocean. Maybe this canal opens into the ocean, and that is where I need to be. Before I can explore more, time runs short, and I am called back to Amen Alley. The service is ending, and we must return to Sugar Grove Plantation.

Ah'Sa Wei

(Golden Fawn)/Rebecca

Once again, the rhythm of my days has changed at Mount Faith Manor. I accompany Isaac into town several times a week to work in the shop on Tudor Street. I enjoy leaving the plantation and learning the ins and outs of importing and exporting. I am amazed at the bigness of the world. We used to trade a few things with other tribes and the Strangers when I lived in *TseNaCoMoCo*, but never in buildings like the ones that line the streets in Bridgetown.

Transactions between the PaTow'O'Mek, other Powhatan tribes or the Strangers took place in our village or at meeting points that were never fixed. We traded antimony, which was a blackish silvery rock that we ground into powder. It was used mostly as face and body paint. It could be mixed with walnut oil or water and had a sheen that made it a desired commodity. Our woven eel traps were sought after as well, and over the years the tribe had developed a reputation for breeding work dogs. We did not keep paper records of our dealings; we remembered the details of who gave what and what was received in return.

This is all so different. Isaac and I have developed an easy rapport and being with him is enjoyable. He has taught me so much.

Until today, we have always taken the same route to and from the plantation to the shop each week.

After our work is concluded on this day, I settle in for the ride back to Mount Faith Manor. Isaac smiles at me and says, "I want to show you something, Miss Rebecca, if you are willing."

I trust him. He has always been respectful and considerate, so I reply, "I am willing, of course."

Instead of turning the Big Dogs toward the east, he leads them northwest and within a few minutes, we are facing the vast ocean, the big water I traveled upon to get to Barbados. Trees grow near the beach, and Isaac ties up the horses and extends his hand to help me. As I step off the carriage, my shoes are quickly covered with sand.

Isaac bends and removes them.

"Feel this with your bare feet, Rebecca." He takes off his shoes, too. The sand is warm from the sun, and standing here with a friend reminds me of home. We are alone, the beach is isolated. Isaac takes off his linen slave trousers and shirt and motions for me to do the same and I follow his lead.

"You must feel the water, Rebecca," he says, and holding my hand, takes me to the water's edge.

The waves lap against my feet, the water warm and inviting. We walk into the gentle surf together. I dive under a wave and come up laughing. I feel almost human again, here in the ocean. Instinctively, I raise my hands to honor the Great Hare, thanking Him for the gift of the sea. Separately, we swim and float but then Isaac moves toward me and we come together for a few minutes or maybe longer, time has ceased to matter.

He holds me in the water, caressing my head. It is tenderness I have not felt in many moons, and I am grateful that these feelings still exist in me. I had started to think I was numb to affection, that part of me having died when the Strangers killed my husband. Maybe I can love again, I am not sure. I have to stay focused on leaving Barbados and getting back home with

MaNa. Isaac and I exit the water, get dressed and start the ride back to our plantation.

After our diversion, we take a different route back to Mount Faith Manor. I am looking out at the unending fields of tall sugar cane, noticing the subtle movement of the leaves on the stalks as the wind blows. Harvest is just beginning and slaves all over the island are working late into the night. In the distance I see the shadow of a crew, methodically cutting the stalks followed by the gathering and hauling to the nearby mill. The red-orange fire glows, and smoke billows into the dusky sky; the now-familiar smell of burning sugar fills the air as we draw closer. I ponder the strange familiarity; something that I knew nothing of just moons ago is now a routine part of my life. From this distance, the slaves look like dancers, moving in unison in their various roles.

One of the women catches my eye. She appears to be taller than her companions or is it that her posture is just more erect? She is dressed as the others, in the traditional slave linen and head wrap. I again realize how fortunate I am to no longer work in the fields, the brutality of cane farming takes so many lives. As we draw closer, I cannot take my eyes off this woman. Why has she captured my attention? Maybe she is one of the PaTow'O'Mek? There are rumors that most of our tribe members have already died in captivity.

My heart starts beating more rapidly, my breathing falters and I grab Isaac's arm, "Take me there!" I say, pointing to the field we are passing.

"What? Nay, we have to get back, Master is expecting us."

"Isaac, nay, stop the cart then, let me off," I am pleading with him. Tears fill my eyes and escape down my cheeks. He maneuvers the carriage to get closer but eventually has to stop and I jump off and run toward the mill.

"NePa'WeXo! Xo!" I call to the figure who I am sure is NePa'WeXo, whom I have not seen since we were sold off the *Trinity* two years ago. She does not hear me at first, but I keep running, stumbling through the harvested field. One by one, the slaves turn from their work to see who is this howling mad woman running toward them. My eyes are glued to her and when she finally turns around, I know I am right.

It takes a second or two for her brain to process what is happening and when she does, she drops the stalks she was holding and begins to run toward me. Her scarf falls off as she runs and when we meet, we cling to one another and drop to our knees embracing. Salty tears are falling and there are no words to describe the happiness that fills my being to know NePa'WeXo is alive.

"WaBus?" I ask. She nods.

"MaNa?" She asks, and I reply, "*BiCi*, yes."

Before we can say more, the foreman from her plantation is upon us with a whip, slashing it through the air. The blow lands on Xo's back but because we are so close together, the last six inches of leather connects with my arm, which swells immediately.

"Get back here, Leah, now!" The foreman bellows as the whip slashes through the air, now finding her neck and shoulder.

We stand and back away from one another, and I realize Isaac is calling my name, "Rebecca!"

Before we turn away from each other. Xo crosses her chest with her hands and mouths the words to me, "*NihTe KihTe'*—my heart, your heart."

She returns to the field, and I walk toward Isaac, my feet heavy as if they were covered in clay, preventing me from leaving, but I am forced to leave anyway.

I learn that Xo is a slave at a large establishment called Sugar Grove Plantation. I am told that her master is cruel and demanding. I revisit our reunion, replaying our words and sharing the miracle that both our daughters are alive. I am filled with gratitude for this gift. Over the next few days, I consider ways to see her again. I am forced to draw Isaac into my confidence, as I am unable to make these plans alone.

While I accompany Isaac into town just once or twice a week, he runs errands to Bridgetown and other plantations almost daily. I now find any excuse to walk by the stables where he cares for the Big Dogs, carts and carriage. I can hardly contain myself as I approach him.

"Good day, Isaac," I try to act nonchalant, but my heart is in my throat as I say, "I was wondering if you could help me and somehow find a way so I can go to Sugar Grove Plantation and see my friend, Xo?"

Isaac looks around to confirm we are alone. "Miss Rebecca, it is dangerous to visit another plantation, especially Sugar Grove." He is cautious because he is smart. He tells me, "We will talk later."

Over the following days on our trips back and forth to Bridgetown, we discuss the options, analyze strategies and try to figure out how to safely plan a visit. There are so many unknowns—has she learned to read English? If not, and I send her a written message, does she have a trusted friend to decipher it for her? My absence would be surely noticed if I left for a few days. What would be the consequences? I ask Isaac to take the long way home next time we work together in Bridgetown but he refuses. He says we are already late, which is true.

When we approach the house, Master White is standing outside. "Isaac, let Rebecca off quickly. Make haste and return to Bridgetown to fetch the midwife, Sarah's time has come. She is having birth pains, they started at midday. She assured me she had plenty of time, but she seems to be in more distress than when ye other children were born."

"Aye, Master White, let me water the horses, and I'll go back to town."

"There's no time!"

I interrupt, "Master White, please allow me to check on Mistress Sarah. I have helped with birth before, back in Virginia." I call my homeland's English name.

I do not wait for an answer and walk past him up the stairs to the sleeping room of my owners. Mistress Sarah is in her bed, flushed and moaning. She grasps my hand. "Something is wrong, Rebecca. This is not like my other babies. Something is wrong!"

I place my hands on her belly as a contraction begins. It is good and strong, but I can feel that the baby is in the wrong position. The child is bottom down instead of headfirst, so the contractions are not moving the baby into the birth canal. I know this situation could result in the death of one or both the mother and baby, depending on how long the labor lasts.

I run back down the stairs. "Master White, there is a PaTow'O'Mek midwife living at Sugar Grove Plantation. It is closer than going to Bridgetown. She can help Mistress Sarah; she delivered many babies in our tribe. Her name is Xo; her English name might be Leah."

Master White looks at me like my hair is on fire. Maybe he is astonished to hear me speaking so boldly. I do not care; I do not want Mistress Sarah or her child to die. Since it became clear she was with child, I have secretly hoped she would focus on her new baby rather than Mary, and I could reclaim my daughter.

"Isaac," he says, "I'll write a letter to Master Lewis at Sugar Grove, and thou shall water the horses—quickly now, to secure the midwife Rebecca speaks of."

I go back into the bedroom to attend Mistress Sarah. I draw close to her and speak directly in her face, which is closer than usual for a slave and Master, but she is distressed from her labor and I want to calm and help her.

"Mistress Sarah, listen to me, I can help you." I place my hands carefully on her shoulders, to settle her spirit.

"There is a midwife at Sugar Grove Plantation. She is from my tribe. She knows what to do. Isaac is going to get her." Between her contractions, I help her to the floor and position her on her hands and knees, demonstrating how to rock her pelvis back and forth. Sometimes this movement will compel a baby to move. When she begins to scream with the next contraction, I show her how to breathe through the pain and to keep her voice low, moaning rather than wailing. We believe this low moan is the sound the earth made as it was being formed by the Great Hare and as we mimic this sound, instead of yelling, labor progresses more steadily. She does as I say and is able to rest between contractions.

When I feel her belly again, I do not think the baby has moved, so I help her to lie on the floor and lift her hips, hoping to move the baby's bottom out of her pelvis. I put pillows under her buttocks to keep her in this position when the next contraction comes.

Time is moving so slowly, and I am beginning to feel a sense of panic when Master White leads Xo into the room. Speaking in our language, I explain that the baby is breech and what I have done, attempting to reposition the fetus. It is so good to speak in our own words again! Xo and I help Mistress Sarah back into the bed; Xo confidently places her hands on Mistress Sarah's swollen abdomen and begins to manually turn the baby. She pushes and pulls. It is painful to Mistress White, and dangerous, but we have limited options.

After what seems an eternity, we see Mistress Sarah's abdomen bulge and roll. Xo's smile confirms the baby has at last turned. Labor progresses more quickly now and a healthy baby boy is safely born to Master Russell and Mistress Sarah White at Mount Faith Manor. We clean mother and baby; the infant hungrily nurses at the breast of his exhausted mother. I have learned from the other slaves to mix lemon juice and molasses into hot water as a tea for postpartum mothers. It helps to restore the blood that was lost during birth. I prepare this drink for Mistress Sarah and then take my leave with Xo.

It is early morning, but still dark outside so I lead Xo to the sleeping quarters for house slaves and we lie quietly, grateful a new life has arrived and giddy to be reunited. As we lie side by side, holding hands, we try to cover all the events that have transpired in our lives since we left the *Trinity*. There is so much to say that much is left unsaid.

When daybreak comes, we part ways, but we know we will be together again. We vow in our PaTow'O'Mek tradition, with one hand over our hearts and the other toward the rising sun, that we will find a way to visit while we remain in Barbados. We also promise each other that we will return to our homeland, somehow, someway, with our daughters in hand.

Ah'SaWei

(Golden Fawn)/Rebecca

In the time that has passed since the Whites' baby arrived, I have been relegated to more work outside the house and thus I see MaNa infrequently. My hopes that the infant would occupy Mistress Sarah's time and that her interest in MaNa would wane have not come to pass. Mistress Sarah has drawn MaNa deeper into her lair along with the new child. A few weeks after the birth, MaNa runs to me when she sees me outside.

"*Nek*! I have a brother!" she exclaims to me as we hug. She goes on to describe this baby boy, unaware that what she is saying pierces my heart, but at this moment I can say nothing to challenge her perception. There is something about her exuberance that warms my heart and her joy about a new baby. I remember my own happiness whenever a new baby was born into the tribe. In spite of everything, I too, am happy for the new life at Mount Faith Manor.

I routinely accompany Isaac and Master White into Bridgetown to assist in the shop. Master White is fond of talking and teaches Isaac and me many things about the Quaker faith, in addition to aspects of the trading business. He explains that the Friends came to Barbados because of persecution in England and that the Jews also came because they were being threatened in Brazil and Portugal. I am fascinated to know that all these people have lived in a world I never knew existed. It is difficult to understand how they have suffered for their beliefs about God and have come to this new place. It is hard for me to imagine ever wanting to leave *TseNaCoMoCo*. I am only here because I was captured and sold as chattel, but many on this island have come of their own accord, seeking freedom. The irony is not lost on me that they came for freedom but have, in turn, enslaved other human beings.

At least once a moon, Isaac and I take the cart from the Whites' Tudor Street shop over to Swan Street to trade with Gomes and Sons. Old Master Gomes' store supplies the island with most of the tools, lumber, iron and so forth needed to keep the sugar mills running. The Gomes men have dark, full beards and wear flowing robes over their breeches. Their apparel is strikingly different from the other shop and plantation owners. We do our bartering with them in English but if we arrive unexpectedly, we hear them speaking a language I have never heard. Isaac says it is Hebrew, the language of the Jewish inhabitants in Barbados.

Levi Gomes is the youngest of the sons. He is always filling orders and loading the carts, but he never does the negotiating; that is for the older brothers or their father. The Jewish community has the same problem that the Anglicans and the Quakers have: there are not enough women for all the men to have a wife. It is a problem that is solved by the taking of enslaved women as companions or common-law wives.

After almost three years in Barbados, I am still not attuned to the nuances of sexual or romantic relationships between the planter class, the merchants and the slaves. I am fortunate to live at Mount Faith Manor, as Master White does not demand to couple with the slave women, and he does not use force. It is clear that many of the plantation owners feel they have a right to have intercourse with their slaves, regardless of the desire of the slave. Xo told me she has been raped many times by Master Lewis.

I have listened to many conversations between the slave women at Mount Faith Manor when no one else is around, discussing marriage, children, freedom. Elizabeth and Ruth joke that they are both too old for such foolishness now. In the kitchen, Betty will say, "Rebecca, there's only one way to get out of here alive, you gone have to marry a white man." And then she cackles at the ridiculousness of what she has just said.

They both know African slaves on other plantations who are living with the sons of the plantation owners. Sometimes the owners will have two wives, a European wife and a slave wife. The slave wife and her children have better quarters than the other slaves. But there are also cautionary tales of slave women who anticipated their freedom after years of companionship and even the birthing of heirs who were later denied their promised free papers. The established religions do not sanction these interracial unions but instead turn a blind eye to them, especially if the appropriate tithes and taxes have been paid.

I say this because Levi has no wife. His mother is dead, so his father is alone as well. One brother has a Jewish wife, familiar with their customs, and the other brother lives with an African slave he owns. When we are trading at Gomes and Sons, Levi is very friendly and has even slipped gifts of hard sugar candy into my pocket or hand. Sometimes he winks one eye at me. I do not know what to think about this, both the candy and the winking, but he seems to have a gentle spirit, so I thank him and privately enjoy the treat once I am back at the plantation.

Isaac is mesmerized by the Jewish cemetery and the Quaker garden burial grounds, two parcels of land that sit side by side near the intersection of Swan and Tudor streets. The garden cemetery has no markers, just areas of newly disturbed dirt amid the flowers, trees, and shrubs. That is the burial tradition of the Friends. It is obvious where bodies have been buried, though; the different stages of vegetation regrowth demonstrate the timelines.

The burial grounds of the Jews are completely different. Large rectangular pieces of granite have been cut and lie on top of the interred remains. The tops of the granite slabs are engraved with the name of the dead, the dates and sometimes a carved picture. The embellishments are most often that of a tree being cut down. Isaac tells me the tree symbolizes the life that is now over, the life cut down from earth and now put into the ground.

Isaac tells me that in Africa, the dead are placed in the ground beneath their huts or in the yard, so the spirit of the deceased knows where he or she is and does not have to roam around the earth looking for home. Isaac often ponders the differences in the faiths; he seems to weigh the various beliefs, trying to discern if one is better than the other. I just listen to him as he thinks out loud, smiling every once in a while so he knows I'm still listening.

We occasionally walk from Swan Street to the Friends garden, noticing if there are new graves. We peek through the foliage to observe the synagogue, the comings and goings of the worshippers. Isaac studies this cemetery as well, wanting to understand the burial customs that are so different from both our native countries and that of the Quakers. In addition to the cemetery, there are three buildings on the property: the large temple for services, a house where the Jewish leader and his family live, and a smaller building. The smaller building is interesting as twice we have seen men exiting it and both times, their beards and hair appeared to be wet. Maybe it is some sort of bathhouse?

Sometimes after these side trips, I think about my husband and how he was so violently killed, his body left to the elements as the women and children were marched to the ocean. I wish I could have prepared him for burial, washed him and braided his hair. I would have placed his bow and mantle beside him and carefully wrapped him in a tanned leather hide. I wish I could have painted my face black, shaved my head and mourned for him, thanking O'Ki'Us for the life we had together. MaMan would have been put into the ground in the forest; there would be no marker. The disturbed earth would have been covered with leaves, camouflaged, to keep animals and evil spirits away. I would have made sure of it. So many memories of him and my former life fill my mind.

"Rebecca," says Isaac softly. "Rebecca," he says again.

"Yes," I reply, returning to the reality of the moment: I am a PaTow'O'Mek slave riding in a horse drawn cart with an African slave on the island of Barbados.

"You were smiling," he says. "Why?"

I cannot help but smile again but feel uncertain about sharing this private memory with Isaac. I look into his face and he smiles warmly in return.

"I was thinking about my husband, MaNa's father. His name was MaMan—it means Bear. He and all the other men in our tribe were killed when the women and children were captured and sold as slaves."

Isaac listens, glancing at me but keeps his eyes on the road.

"I was smiling because I remembered a time when I put a thin green snake in my ear lobe instead of an earring. I was still a child; it was before my first blood. I was copying my older brother who had done a similar thing."

Isaac looks perplexed, so I go on with the story.

"On that day when I was merrily imitating my brother's mischievousness, I happened to see MaMan as he was returning to our village after a day of hunting. He later told me that when he saw me playing and laughing with a live snake in my ear, he knew he wanted me for his wife once I was old enough."

I suddenly feel shy, telling this intimate detail of my life.

There is silence for a bit, and then Isaac says, "I can understand why he wanted to marry you."

I know only that Isaac once had a wife and that she lived on another plantation. She died in childbirth as did the baby and he never got to see her or the baby before they were put in the ground.

He has suffered loss, as we all have. I do not know how to respond to his statement, so I smile and reach for his hand and momentarily hold it. I have found that the holding of another's hand, be it in death or birth or friendship, is comforting and communicates in a way that words cannot.

Xo

(Shining Moon)/Leah

Since I assisted with the successful delivery of Mistress White's baby, midwifery duties have been added to my list of chores at Sugar Grove Plantation. Master Lewis now demands that I provide care to the pregnant slaves when their times come. That is fine by me; I like the work. When I am with a laboring woman, helping bring new life into the world, I always think of my own baby, my son, taken from my arms as we were marched toward the *Trinity*. I yearn to see him and hold him again, even as I know he is no longer a baby and likely does not even remember me.

I have also been hired out to other nearby plantations to help with slave deliveries. Master Lewis is paid for my services, but he has never compensated me in any way. I carry with me a vast body of knowledge and experience that came from my mother, grandmother and the other women in *TseNaCoMoCo*. While Master Lewis defers to me in this area, he remains a tyrant and demands the new mothers here at his plantation get back into the field or to their responsibilities in the main house immediately. He has no understanding that a woman should rest until her post-delivery bleeding lessens and that nursing a new baby is vital in the first days in order for the milk to come in plentifully. He is cruel in every way when it comes to the treatment of his slaves. So many die here that he frequently has to buy replacements at the market in Bridgetown.

Mistress Lewis is again with child. As her belly grows bigger with the pregnancy, Master Lewis' sexual appetites became even more voracious. All the women on the plantation try to give him a wide berth to avoid his vicious "business." I am the object of his lascivious desire most often, so much so that he has even asked me, "How are you not with child, Leah? I would like to see what kind of bastard you would give me." He is oblivious to the needs of others, in part because of his chronic drunkenness. He never even guesses that I have been pregnant with his child.

At some point, he tells me he is not going to pay for the English midwife to come care for Mistress Lewis when she delivers. "Why should I pay someone else, when I have you?"

I knew instinctively that this was a terrible idea and that Mistress Lewis would not want to be assisted at birth by a woman her husband was routinely raping. Her jealous raging had been muted as her pregnancy progressed, but she was livid on the day she delivered when Master Lewis would not call for the English midwife. He roughly pulled me up the stairs by the arm and shoved me into her room, closing the door behind me.

"I hate you!" She yells to him as she flings a crystal water glass at the closed door where it shatters. Then to me she screams, "I hate you, too! I do not want you here! Leave! Now!"

Her contractions are already very close, and her tirade is cut short as another pain silences her wailing. She does not speak to me after this outburst, but she accepts my assistance as she labors, tears rolling down her cheeks. Mistress Lewis is strong, and her baby girl arrives safely.

All she says afterwards is, "I hoped it would be a boy."

Mistress Lewis has now delivered her fourth child, so there are three daughters and one son in the Lewis family. WaBus is charged with tending the new baby. One of the African slaves is the child's wet nurse. The slave suckles two infants, her own, also a child of Master Lewis, and the baby he produced with his wife.

I cannot help but think relationships would be simpler in Barbados if the English treated physical intimacy as we did in *TseNaCoMoCo*. If a married person wished to couple with someone besides their husband or wife, the matter was discussed without emotion and permission usually granted. If the husband or wife had intercourse without permission, however, the offending man was put to death. So in our tribe, if Master Lewis did not ask his wife and receive permission for his liaisons, he would be killed.

Perhaps if they could have this conversation, Mistress Lewis would agree for Master Lewis to have other partners, and she would not feel so angry about it. I do not know if it would work in Barbados, but the existing system is damaging to everyone. The babies and children suffer at the hand of Mistress Lewis when she sees them in the garden or in their huts. She has been known to pinch them until blood is drawn, slap and violently push the mulatto slave progeny. They are innocent, but they suffer the most, easily identifiable as children with mixed blood, obviously spawned by Master Lewis.

WaBus, Anne, has not yet experienced her first blood, but it is clear that she is maturing and that becoming a woman will happen within the next year. It worries me tremendously, and I encourage her to be wary around Master Lewis and stay away from the main house as much as possible. The wet nurse lives in one of the huts closer to the sugar fields, so WaBus watches the baby there much of the time under the guise of keeping her fed. Mistress Lewis has very little interest in her fourth child and has taken to her bed with what the English call a case of melancholy.

Mistress and Master Lewis fight often, loudly and physically with Master Lewis ultimately striking his wife once or twice. She attempts to physically fight him, but he is stronger. When he lands a blow, the altercation usually ends. The fighting always erupts after

Master Lewis has been drinking sugar wine, and since he drinks daily, the outbursts are frequent. This kind of fighting is unusual for the PaTow'O'Mek. We settle differences calmly by talking between ourselves or having other tribe members mediate any misunderstandings. The violent ways of the English are quite unsettling.

In the midst of one of those fights, I hear Master Lewis tell his wife that he plans to go to the New World to visit his brother who grows tobacco. His brother has become a successful plantation owner and Master Lewis wants to see how wealthy his brother has become. I am in the washroom, scrubbing dirty linens, and Master Lewis stands in the courtyard yelling his plans to Mistress Lewis's second floor bedroom window. When he is finished, he looks my way, but I pretend to be oblivious to the conversation.

I do not know what transpired between them but within the next week, Mistress Lewis announces that she and the children, all four of them, will accompany Master Lewis on his trip to the New World to visit his brother. It is WaBus who tells me that the plans are formalized because she is to accompany the Lewises on this trip, to care for the children. WaBus still has vivid, horrifying memories of our trip across the water on the *Trinity*. She is apprehensive about being away from me and my protection. She is intuitive enough to know that Master Lewis is watching her. The thought of being separated from my daughter shakes me to my core, and I am desperate to devise a plan to prevent this from happening. What are my options?

Over the next days, I ponder every scenario: I could kill Master Lewis as he does his business with me, thus canceling the trip, but I would likely be put to death immediately, leaving WaBus alone and vulnerable without me. I can send her away into hiding, perhaps to Mount Faith Manor where Ah'SaWei could watch over her, but again, if discovered, the ramifications would be deadly. Could I somehow ingratiate myself to Master Lewis to accompany the family as additional slave labor? After all, they will need food to be prepared, necessary pots emptied, clothes washed. How can I broach this subject with him? I know that Mistress Lewis will not want me near her husband, but it is also clear that she wields no power over him.

The next time Master Lewis comes to me for coupling, I do not resist, I do not turn my head away in disgust. When he finishes, he says, "Well, Leah, after all this time, you have no fight left? I hope you are not sick. Are you? Sick, that is?" he asks, as he buttons his breeches.

Deep inside I am seething, but I need him now, so I have to be careful with my words. I do not know enough of the English language and as a slave and as a woman, I cannot fully engage him in a conversation. The trip is getting closer every day, so I just blurt out, "Take me with you."

He regards me with shock, as if I were a talking dog or a rock that suddenly spoke to him. He moves closer to the door of the hut without responding.

"You need slaves in addition to Anne," I start, using her English name, "for the trip and later at your brother's house. You know I can wash and cook. Someone will need to empty the chamber pots. I know how to do this work," my pleas roll out of my mouth like a rushing stream.

"No," he says, as he opens the door. "I will take the wet nurse; she also knows how to do the other work." He has already thought about this.

"But she has her own baby—"

"Her baby will stay here; there are other slaves who can provide milk." He is heartless to think of separating a newborn from its mother.

I know I am acting recklessly, but I have no choice. I lower my eyes and say, "I am the only one who knows how to heal when there is sickness in addition to doing the other work. I took care of the sick slaves and sailors on board the *Trinity*." I wait with my head bowed and brace myself, expecting to be slapped.

He leaves without uttering another word. I slide to the dirt floor, my mind racing for other solutions. There are only two thoughts now: I must get WaBus to Mount Faith Manor to hide shortly before the Lewises depart. The timing will be critical, as once their plans are set and the dates chosen, the ship will not wait just for them; there will be other considerations.

Secondly, I contemplate the likelihood of success were I to sneak aboard the sailing vessel and hide for the duration of the trip. If I conceal myself within the cargo hold, perhaps WaBus could secretly bring me enough food and water so I could survive the journey. But once we arrive in the New World, then what?

I am running in the snow, away from something terrible. I am near the creek in TseNaCoMoCo, and it is frozen over. I am wearing my white slave clothes, but my feet are bare. I try to look over my shoulder as I run to see what is chasing me, but I cannot tell what it is because of the thick falling snow. It is a beast of some sort, and it is gaining on me, so I run onto the frozen ice, slipping and falling to my knees and sliding further from the shore. The ice cracks and I am suddenly flailing through the frigid shards, sinking to the bottom.

I look up, through the water and the hole in the ice above me. The beast is a hairy wild boar with long curled tusks, his breath puffing out in white clouds from his snout and mouth. The animal and I stare at each other until it walks away. As I lie sprawled on the bottom of the creek, I close my eyes.

I am tormented even in my sleep.

Xo
(Shining Moon)/Leah

S laves are packing the trunks for the trip to the New World. The upcoming voyage has rejuvenated Mistress Lewis, and she is animated as she orders the slaves to prepare clothes and non-perishable food items for the journey. The dressmaker has been here for a week, sewing new clothes for the children, anticipating the cooler temperatures in Virginia. Yes, Master Lewis's brother lives in Virginia—my *TseNaCoMoCo*!

When I learn that this is their destination, my plans are solidified. I will sneak aboard the ship, hide myself with the cargo, and get back home to my son and any remnant of the tribe that might be left. WaBus does not know of my plan yet; I do not want her compromised in any way with the knowledge. I have complete confidence in her ability to smuggle occasional food tidbits to keep me alive. Since WaBus and the wet nurse will travel with the family as slaves to provide help on the journey, the seamstress has made them each a coat and a dress with a petticoat for warmth. Leather shoes have been ordered from the cobbler in Bridgetown. There is an air of excitement at Sugar Grove Plantation that I have not witnessed before.

I try to appear blank; I do not want my emotions to give me away. I go about my jobs, washing clothes, delivering babies, tending to the slaves in the sick house. Master Lewis has not come to me for his "business" since I begged to accompany the family. It is most assuredly a relief, but I wonder what changed his attitude? Was it my lack of resistance the last time or was it my asking to come along? I do not know. Maybe he is just distracted due to all the details of the trip. Maybe he is biding his time, plotting to assault WaBus once she is away from me. I cannot even think about such a thing happening. I have to stay focused on my plan.

I steal pieces of men's clothing when I am called to neighboring plantations for midwifery duties. I always carry a satchel containing items to help with deliveries, and there is room to slip a pair of breeches or a blouse into the bottom of the bag. I even lifted a hat from the alley one Sunday as we stood outside for church. I spied it left behind on the floor of a cart that brought worshippers and slaves to Saint Michael's Cathedral. I grabbed it and shoved it under my blouse. No one was the wiser. Then I walked to the docks to look at the ships, as was my usual Sunday practice. I never stand in the alley listening to the Anglican service.

I can see that I am as tall or slightly taller than most of the Englishmen on the island. If I am careful, I can camouflage myself as a man and walk right onto the ship, then slip into the cargo hold once on board. I ponder the best time, likely at dusk. In my musings, I realize I do not smell as foul as most of the men, might that give me away? I check my hidden articles of clothing, smelling them. They are mostly clean. I plan to layer them on top of my slave linens, to give the appearance of more bulk. Master Lewis has several flasks that he always carries, imbibing throughout the day on sugar wine. When he leaves one in the stable, I surreptitiously cover it with my hand and palm the prize, again hiding it in my blouse. I cannot even fathom how I will use it or if I will need it, but the imbibing of sugar wine seems to be a manly habit in Barbados. As I watch the men more closely to hone my imitation, I feel the flask may be useful somehow. Maybe I will just spill some of the contents on my clothing for the smell.

A caretaker will live at Sugar Grove Plantation while the Lewises are away. I meet him and immediately distrust him. I am not sure why; perhaps he is a thief or maybe worse. I am told to help him manage the day-to-day life on the plantation. Master Lewis gratuitously flatters me with his words, telling the man, "Leah is very smart. If you have questions, she can help you." Little does he know I will not be here but I nod, implying my acquiescence.

The ship that will sail to Virginia is called the *Mermaid*. WaBus writes out the letters on a slip of paper and I memorize them. I look at the paper many times a day so I can recognize the shapes. I finally tell her my plan because the family and slaves will board the *Mermaid* within the next two days. All I can say is that I will also be on board, in the cargo area, hiding, and that she should look for me.

My little WaBus, not so little anymore, hugs me when I tell her. Did she ever doubt I would leave her or let her go without me? Her countenance is so light after this that I fear Master or Mistress Lewis will detect the change and become suspicious, but they are so consumed by their own affairs that they pay no attention to the heart of their slave girl.

As the family leaves, I cling to my WaBus as if I would never see her again. While my plan is to join her, there are no guarantees that I will be successful.

I whisper to her, "We will find your brother; we will be free once more." We touch foreheads and noses. We each place a hand to our heart and the other hand lifted to the Gods, whoever the God may be: the Great Hare, O'Ki'Us, Jesus of the Anglicans and Quakers or Yahweh of the Jews. Our unspoken promise is to be together again soon. I watch as she disappears down the wet lane.

I have only briefly seen Ah'SaWei after realizing the Lewises were going to the New World and taking WaBus with them. I had hoped to hide WaBus at Mount Faith Manor, but the situation there was dire as well. Ah'SaWei told me the Whites were attempting to adopt MaNa. We again pledged to do all we could to return to our homeland and be reunited there. I know that once I get back to *TseNaCoMoCo*, find my son, and maybe even my brother, I will do everything in my power to get Ah'SaWei and MaNa back to our tribal lands, too. I do not know how it will unfold. At this point, I live hour by hour.

The timing is critical; I cannot leave the plantation too soon, but I also have to get into Bridgetown before the *Mermaid* sets sail. My disguise is hidden in my midwifery bag, along with an apple, three pieces of dried pork and the flask of sugar wine. I know the road to Bridgetown. I will walk it during the night, hiding in the ditches and gullies along the way if necessary.

Just as I am about to leave, there is a knock on the door. But before I can answer, it opens. It is the hired overseer. My heart sinks, anticipating his motive for coming to my hut.

"Leah," he says, "why don't you join me for some refreshment—the big house is quiet now that the family is gone."

I shake my head, but he says, "Come along now, be a good girl. I don't want to hurt you." He holds the door open and motions for me to exit and I do. As I pass him, I recognize the familiar, sickening smell of Master Lewis when he was drunk. My mind is racing. How can I avoid whatever he is planning?

He leads me into the big house to the dining room table. I have never been in here except to serve, and now he tells me, "Sit. I hear you savages go crazy and cannot handle firewater, sugar wine, rum, whatever they call it here. I would like to see this for myself. Here you go."

He pours and hands me a small glass of liquid from the crystal decanter. He pours one for himself and says, "Cheers, drink up."

He swallows his in one gulp and I stare at my glass. I have never had more than a spoonful of sugar wine. I do not like the taste of it. I have seen how it changes people when too much is consumed.

He slaps the table with his palm, rattling the glass and the candelabra. "Now!"

I drink it, slowly. It burns as I swallow. He refills our glasses and downs his. I just look at my glass.

"Now, girl, come along, quickly," he urges.

I do not want to do this; I need to get to Bridgetown.

He grabs me by the hair, pulling my head back and pours the intoxicating liquid in my mouth. I gag, some of the wine spilling down the front of my blouse, but most of it goes down my throat. He is rough now, all pretense of friendliness gone. He takes a swig straight from the decanter and hands it to me. I bring the container to my mouth, pretending to drink but let most of the wine fall from my lips onto my clothes. I hope he will not notice, but of course he does, and he becomes enraged at my attempted deception.

I feel the effects of the liquor, dizzy and unbalanced. I know where this is going. He tells me to dance. He says he wants to see how savages dance. I cannot think clearly, but I need to be done with this. I need to leave this abominable place, this evil island. I stand on unsteady feet and begin to move as he has demanded and that is all it takes. He tackles me to the dining room floor and the assault is over quickly. He passes out and I roll him off me. He is unconscious.

I run for the back door and my hut. My living companions silently assess my condition and watch as I grab my satchel and leave. They will not betray me; they have not been told anything. For their protection and for mine, I have shared my plans with no one. Once outside the door, nausea overwhelms me and I vomit near the threshold, a parting gift for Sugar Grove Plantation.

This turn of events was unexpected, and yet somehow nothing ever surprises me now. I am steadfast and march toward Bridgetown. Nausea washes over me occasionally, but I keep walking. I am ready to slip into the ditch at the slightest sound or glimmer of light. Mercifully, the night is clear, and the moon alone brightens the path to freedom. I am accompanied only by the songs of the cicadas. At some point, I leave the road and put on my stolen trousers and shirts on top of my slave garb. I twist my braid and cover it with a bandana and put on the man's hat. That is all I can do. I have to smile—between the spilled sugar wine and the vomit, I smell quite manly.

When I get to the wharf, I have a momentary sense of panic. There are so many ships and not all of them are docked on shore. Some are anchored in the bay and will require passage on a dinghy, like the one that took us to the *Trinity*.

I remember back to that day, it seems a lifetime ago, when I realized WaBus and I were being rowed out to a larger ship, away from *TseNaCoMoCo* and away from my baby boy, Strong Son. At that time, I impulsively decided to jump off the small boat and swim back to shore, grabbing WaBus by the hand and yelling, "*TaMoKin*! Swim!"

Although we were recaptured, I felt at peace knowing I had tried everything possible to avoid leaving my son.

The sun is rising as I walk along the docks, looking for the markings that will reveal the names of the ships. There are a few people milling about, including some drunken sailors, so at that moment I decide to play the part of an inebriated deck hand trying to find my way back to my ship. I hang my head, walking slowly, occasionally missing a step just in case someone is watching.

Most of the ship names are painted on the bows, but the lettering is not straightforward. There are flourishes that make deciphering the words confusing to me. After passing so many, I am resigned to accepting my faulty plan, and then, as if O'Ki'Us has willed it, there is the *Mermaid*.

The carved decoration at the front of the ship is that of a woman, her naked breasts exposed, her hair flowing and, below the waist instead of legs, she appears to be a fish with scales and a tail. Ah, of course the figurehead on the *Mermaid* would be that of a mermaid! In my years in Barbados, I have heard of the superstitions of sailors and their legends, one of those being that semi-naked figures of women carved on the front of ships could calm the storms at sea.

The gangplank is in place and sailors are already bustling about on deck. My heart is beating so hard, I can hear it in my ears, but I amble across the makeshift bridge as if I belong there and no one says a word. On board at last, I look for the hatch that will lead to the cargo and below decks.

It is already propped open. I stumble toward the hatch and fall into the hole. Like a chased rat, I scramble as far as I can go, hiding myself in the deep recesses behind the barrels. I am on the *Mermaid*. I am on my way home!

As relief floods my being, I wonder, is my daughter somewhere on this ship?

I am standing in a gulley in the jungle, looking at the entrance to a cave. There is movement and a Big Dog emerges from the dark space. As this Big Dog, this horse, comes forward, I see it has giant wings that flutter open. It is magnificent! There is a woman on the horse. It is KeSaTo! My mother! I run to her and she somehow lifts me up onto the horse's back to ride with her. I put my arms around her waist and feel so much joy. I have missed her.

The horse flaps its wings and begins to fly. I cling to my mother, afraid of falling but very happy to be with her. She does not speak but she keeps looking back at me, smiling. She is young and healthy, the way she looked before she got sick. The horse is taking us over the ocean, I can see islands and water. The water is endless. I finally see land and the horse begins to descend but then he dips his head and my mother and I slide off. We are falling through the air, I am terrified.

My mother is holding my hands as we fall and she says, "You are fine, NePa'WeXo. You are safe." Our hands slip apart and she disappears upward into the clouds as I plummet toward the earth.

Ah'SaWei
(Golden Fawn)/Rebecca

So many changes are taking place in Barbados, or at least in my little world on the island. Gomes and Sons are planning to move their business to the New World, a place called New York. They are selling most of their inventory to Master White, so Isaac and I have been going into Bridgetown more frequently to help transfer items from Gomes and Sons on Swan Street to the Whites' shop on Tudor Street.

The English government here is attempting to pass laws forbidding Jews from owning slaves. Jews have already lost the right to own sugar plantations and now will have no labor. Old Master Gomes is a reserved man, but the pressure of relocating seems to be weighing on him and he speaks harshly to his sons. There is a lot of tension in the shop. Isaac and I try to stay focused on our jobs at the moment. As we are preparing to transfer a cart load of goods, Levi steps out of Gomes and Sons and says, "Can I ride along?"

Obviously, he can do as he wishes. He is a free man, and while the rights of the Jews on Barbados are being eroded, he is still un-shackled, while Isaac and I are slaves.

"Of course, Master Levi, you are welcome to come with us," says Isaac. I am about to climb into the back of the cart with the tools and wood when Levi motions for me to just slide over on the bench.

I am now tucked between Isaac and Levi for the short ride. Levi is not one to stand on ceremony, but I know this is highly improper, and it makes me feel uneasy.

When we get to the shop Levi says, "Isaac, I need to have a word with Miss Rebecca. Go ahead and unload; we'll return shortly."

Isaac and I look at each other, dumbfounded and speechless. I allow myself to be led along Tudor Street toward the water. When we get to the docks, ships are coming and going in addition to the ones securely anchored. We stand together, facing the vast ocean lost in our own thoughts for a moment.

Then Levi says, "Come with me to the New World, Rebecca. Be my wife and let us start anew. I will buy you from Mount Faith Manor and once we arrive in New York, I will emancipate you. I will teach you the ways of Judaism, we will worship Yahweh together and grow a large family."

He stops and laughs softly before he continues. "I have seen that you are loyal, smart and hardworking, as I am. We will make a great marriage and have a satisfying life together, Yahweh willing."

I am flabbergasted. This is unexpected. Yes, we have developed a friendship but—but what?

"I have a child here, Master Levi. I have a daughter, Mary, MaNa. I cannot leave her." I stammer, but this is the most important thing for him to know about me.

"I know about Mary, but the Whites wish to adopt her. It is common knowledge, they plan to make her their own child and heir, legally, and give her all the advantages, including freedom," he says, not realizing the words are like a poison arrow to my spirit.

I, too, have heard the rumors and have ignored the hints dropped by Master and Mistress White. My MaNa still has a living mother, a mother who loves her and wishes to be with her and carry on the traditions of the PaTow'O'Mek with her. My heart is in my throat.

I do not want to show my raw emotions, so I struggle to calmly say, "I will not leave without Mary."

Master Levi is kind and generous, his intentions are genuine, and he does not miss a beat when he responds, "So be it. I will buy Mary, too. We will start our new life together as a family of three."

Although I have not answered him, it appears to be decided. Levi smiles and takes me by the elbow, and we walk back toward the shop.

I am not privy to the negotiations because, in the eyes of the law, I am not a human, I am a thing, a commodity to be bought or sold. Old Master Gomes makes the offer to buy me and Mary directly to Master White, while at the shop in Bridgetown. When Master White gets home and tells his wife, she begins wailing. I can hear her cries coming from the upstairs sleeping chambers even though I am in the detached kitchen below.

"Russell, husband, what can thou be thinking? I will not let Mary go. I cannot lose another child. I will not allow this sale to happen. Mary is mine now, ours, a part of our family. We can give her a much better life than if she returns to the New World. That place is unsafe, untamed—" Her words turn to uncontrollable sobbing.

I cannot hear how Master White responds to his wife's distress. She is inconsolable with the thought of losing her Mary, my MaNa and will not agree to the sale. The Whites do agree, however, to sell me. I do not know how much Levi and his father have to pay for me. I am to live and work at Mount Faith Manor until it is time to board the ship for New York. Aye, Elizabeth was right to warn me about the plans the Whites had for my daughter.

I am careful in my conversations with my daughter as Mistress Sarah is very perceptive and MaNa is an oblivious pawn in this scenario. I take advantage of the fact that I will be leaving to seize every moment possible with her. No one has the audacity to deny me these fleeting minutes with my child. When we are alone, though, I attempt to plant the seed in her head that someday we will be together again. By English accounting, Mary is now six years old. She is still an innocent child and to be sure, she has thrived here at Mount Faith Manor. The love showered on her by Mistress Sarah in addition to my presence has allowed her to heal and forget the horror of the massacre and subsequent voyage on the *Trinity*.

I am grateful that she is strong and resilient, these are characteristics of the PaTow'O'Mek people, and she is undeniably PaTow'O'Mek.

And then there is Isaac. He is as close a friend as I have in Barbados. He is resigned when he hears about the sale and that I will be leaving. We have not consummated our relationship physically. I guess I have been in mourning, not just for MaMan, my beloved husband, but also for my brother and my mother and the loss of my community when all the men in our tribe were slaughtered that night.

I witnessed the horrible deaths of Eightyseven, Eightyeight and Ninety on the Trinity and have seen the degradation of slaves all over Barbados. Living through these events has changed me. I have not been able to give myself to Isaac, but he has been a faithful friend, patiently waiting for me to receive his affection and comfort. Now the threat of losing my daughter weighs heavily on me. Neither Isaac nor I try to put our feelings into words. It is pointless. We are powerless.

The Whites mean well in their way. I see that, but I cannot abide by it. Mistress Sarah said I can have a special dinner with Mary on the night before I leave. MaNa typically eats with the family while I have my meals with the other house slaves. Since I have been offered this opportunity, I decide to have a picnic with MaNa at the edge of the plantation, where the sugar cane fields meet the jungle. When Mistress Sarah asks me about it, I tell her, just a simple meal outside on a blanket.

She replies, "That sounds perfect! Master White and I, along with the baby, will join thee and Mary. I'll have a bountiful picnic prepared."

My vision was to be alone with my daughter for just an hour or so. I want to speak to her of our homeland, talk to her in our language, away from listening ears. I need to make sure she understands that she belongs with me.

Rainy season has begun in Barbados, and water pours from the sky all afternoon, thwarting the planned picnic. I have packed a small bag for the journey to New York. I have very few belongings, just my two linen slave blouses and skirts. I have also placed a few bananas and some nuts in the bottom of my bag. Levi's sister-in-law is gathering two dresses and a pair of shoes for me to wear once I am free and we are on board the *Saint Helene*, the ship that will carry us to the New World.

We eat our picnic dinner inside at the regular dining table, and I am invited to join the family because, after all, I am now technically free; the money for my purchase was exchanged earlier today. Tomorrow morning early, Isaac will take me to Levi and we will leave shortly thereafter. Mistress Sarah is talking too much, trying to ignore the fact that I am leaving. I feel like I am outside my body, watching an unbelievable story unfold.

At last the awkward meal is complete, and all I can muster to say to the Whites is, "Please take good care of my Mary, my MaNa," as I hug my child.

As Mistress White stands and reaches for Mary, I regain my composure and say, "I wish to have a moment with Mary and then I will take my leave."

Without waiting for permission, I take MaNa by the hand and lead her toward the kitchen and through the backdoor. The rain has ceased for a minute and dusk is falling, the frogs are croaking loudly. I walk toward the stables and when we get there, I kneel down to be on her level, so we may look at each other eye to eye. Holding her hand to my chest I say, "MaNa, *NihTe KihTe*', my heart, your heart, my darling girl."

Her eyes fill with tears. Of course, she knows I am leaving tomorrow, but she is confused. Mistress Sarah has minimized my sale and what it really means for my daughter.

I say to her, "I want to tell you a secret, dear MaNa. Can you keep a secret?"

She nods.

"Since we did not get to have our picnic dinner, I will come to you very quietly tonight and we will have midnight dessert under the stars. We will have sugar custards, your favorite. Does that sound like fun?"

She nods again.

"But this is a secret, just for us. When I come to get you for dessert, you must be very quiet, even if you are sleepy, do you understand?" My voice is shaking as I whisper to her. I am trembling as I return to standing and again take my daughter's hand.

I know that if we stay too long, Mistress Sarah will come looking for us. With that, we return to the big house. I hug my daughter for what is to be the last time and watch her as she goes upstairs to prepare for bed.

I have already said my farewells to the other slaves at Mount Faith Manor. I will miss Isaac and Elizabeth. They are my closest friends here; so many others have died. Betty smiles when she hears the news of my sale, "You gone be free girl, you gone be free."

I have frequently sought out Elizabeth because of our shared history on the *Trinity*. Her health is failing, and she has a cough that is worsening by the day.

We embrace tightly and she says only, "Be careful." Her intuition is infallible; I know that to be true. She and Isaac are happy for me. If one slave is freed, it keeps hope alive for everyone.

I am restless waiting for midnight to arrive. I have already stowed my belongings in the cart. If my things are discovered, I can easily say I packed them because of the early hour the trip is scheduled. I move through the dark night; the clouds have graciously blocked the moonlight so I can approach the house as an unseen shadow. I stand near the back steps, waiting to hear the twelve chimes of the large grandfather clock, and then I will enter the house.

I am strangely calm as I tiptoe up the steps to MaNa's room. She is asleep, as I expected. I gently take her hand and she opens her eyes. I pantomime "shhhh" to her, but I smile broadly to indicate this is the fun midnight dessert escapade I spoke of earlier.

We are down the stairs and out the back door in a matter of minutes. I cannot put my guard down. There are miles to go before we are safely out of this country. Isaac waits with the horse cart, already out of the stable. Neither Isaac nor the horse needs light. They have been down this road thousands of times.

As we turn the corner off of the Mount Faith Manor grounds, MaNa's voice rings out, breaking our furtive silence, "Where are the custards, Rebecca?"

"We will have our treats soon, very soon. We just have a little farther to go," I tell her. "Rest, daughter, I will awaken you when we are there."

We get to Gomes and Sons without incident, and as we arrive at the front door of the shop, Levi steps out from the shadows to meet us. There is no time for pleasantries or belabored goodbyes. Isaac lifts my sleeping daughter from the cart and puts her in my arms.

"Godspeed," is all he says.

I reach for his hand and draw it to my heart in gratitude. He has taken another risk, and it could prove deadly to him. "And to you," I say.

We all know how dangerous this is so MaNa, Levi and I quickly disappear into the nearly empty shop, and Isaac heads back to Mount Faith Manor, swallowed into the dark night.

No one else has been brought into our confidence because it is too risky. None of Levi's family knows of our plans to include my daughter in this new life. They just expect me to board the *Saint Helene* with them and head for a fresh start in New York in the morning. Even Levi and I had not fully planned it, just loosely hoping to hide in the warehouse or store until boarding the *Saint Helene*. Once aboard, I hoped to hide MaNa until we were safely out to sea.

For Isaac, the plan was for him to be back at the stables and sleeping well before daybreak and then to plead ignorance concerning our disappearance. MaNa and I huddle in a dark corner of the empty shop. Levi leaves us so his absence will not arouse suspicion.

In desperation, I pray to the Great Hare, to O'Ki'Us, to Jesus and his father God, Yahweh. Praying for safety for Isaac, for my child to be protected and allowed to be with me and that Levi will come to no harm for his role in this escape.

Unbelievably to me, I have closed my eyes and actually slept for a few minutes or maybe longer. I hear a commotion in the street. Old Master Gomes is speaking loudly to someone—is it Master White? I have so rarely heard Master White angry that his voice is unfamiliar. It is early, earlier than our absence should have been noticed. I feel a sense of panic that the plan is unraveling.

I am a trapped animal with my baby, waiting to be slaughtered when suddenly Levi appears, picks up MaNa, grabs my hand and leads us down a hall to the rear door. We exit silently and run down the alley, hugging the side of the building for cover. I realize we are heading in the direction of the synagogue and burial grounds. I am unnerved as I hear voices and Big Dogs gaining on us. We are momentarily standing in plain view. My mind flashes to the image of Eightyseven as she stood alone on the deck of the *Trinity* just before being shot and killed.

As we enter the grounds, Levi runs toward the smaller building. He quickly opens the door and bolts it behind us. He silently motions for me to follow, as he still carries MaNa. We round a tight corner and there are narrow stone steps leading down into a dark space.

"The mikvah," he whispers. "No one will come in here. This is the sacred bathing pool."

I stand petrified, the small area is filled with water. "You have to hide in here Rebecca; you and Mary must stay here. Get in the water until I come for you."

He sees my fear. "Do not worry. The Rabbi will not permit anyone to come in here to look for you. It is forbidden."

He hands my daughter to me and at his urging I walk down

the steps into the cool water. It is dark, I find a spot in the corner, hoping to become invisible and Levi disappears.

Soon, I hear Levi speaking and denying any knowledge of my whereabouts and even boldly proclaiming, "My father paid for Rebecca! I expect her to be delivered as promised!"

My dear child has retreated into her mute world, the place in her mind where she lived aboard the *Trinity* when the trauma was too much to bear. She begins to shiver from the cold in spite of being held next to me. I am now shivering, too; the moving water has chilled us both.

I hear the door open, and I accept that I will die right now in this place, but I am at peace. I tried to escape, and I will face death bravely with my daughter at my side. I close my eyes; I do not want to watch what happens next.

There is silence so I open my eyes and relief floods my being. It is Levi.

"Rebecca, Master White has searched the *Saint Helene* and he has stationed himself at the ship to watch for you and Mary. My father is now aware of what is happening but is sympathetic to your suffering. He understands the love of a mother for her child. A horse drawn cart will arrive near the mikvah with a large empty trunk. You and Mary will be transported to the ship as cargo and put in the hold. Do not fear. Just move quickly."

He disappears again.

And that is how MaNa and I leave Barbados, packed into a trunk and placed in the cargo hold of the *Saint Helene*, a ship designed to transport people and goods. It struck me as oddly poetic, that we would leave in a similar fashion as we had arrived, considered less than human, and this time, packed in a crate.

Ah'SaWei

(Golden Fawn)/Rebecca

AUTUMN, 1669

NEW YORK

It is *TaQuiTock*, the Time for Gathering Nuts and Hunting Deer. I can tell by the feel of the air on my skin, by the position of the moon, the rising and setting of the sun. But we do not gather nuts or hunt deer here in New York like the PaTow'O'Mek did in *TseNaCoMoCo*. I am living a completely different life, here with my husband Levi, my daughter and Levi's larger family. It feels like home in a way that Barbados never did.

Although New York is an island, the mainland is near and it is all a part of what the Gomes men call the New World. It is new only to the Strangers. This land has been here forever, inhabited by many tribes since the creation of the world. Old Master Gomes catches me smiling when they are talking about this "New World." I think that he can read my mind; he knows this land is not new.

He smiles back at me, then wipes off the smile and resumes his sober conversation. I learn so much when I listen to the men discussing their business, the politics of trading, and the persecution they escaped. Old Master Gomes is the only one who realizes I am listening, except for Levi, of course.

Our village is called *MaNaHahTaAn*, named by the Lenape people who live near us. New York is unlike the island of Barbados in terms of climate and the way it is governed. It is much colder than I remember *TseNaCoMoCo* in the Time for Gathering Nuts. I wonder if it is actually colder, or is it because I have lived in the constant heat of Barbados for the past three years? I prefer this cold because it also feels like freedom. I think I will always associate heat with oppression. My mind is filled with thoughts about everything.

The English control New York, just like they did in Barbados, but with an appointed Governor and then what we would call lesser chiefs. Even though the English kings and governors made the rules in Barbados, they are not the same as the laws here. Most importantly for the Gomes family, there are no laws that discriminate against the Jews. Old Master Gomes and his sons have gone into business with one of his cousins who came here escaping persecution in Brazil a few years earlier. They trade in animal fur: fox, bear, raccoon, but mostly beaver.

The local tribes supply the various types of fur and in exchange receive knives, axes, needles, and glassware. Beaver pelts are considered the best as they have two layers of hair, with long hair on top and then an under layer of shorter hair. The fur is shipped across the ocean where the English and other Europeans use it to embellish their woolen coats with cuffs and collars. Coats can also be lined with fur for extra warmth or even made completely of fur.

I do not work in the Gomes fur trading shop in New York. I stay in our dwelling with my sister-in-law, Esther, and we prepare food for the whole family and take care of MaNa. After we move into our house and start to get settled, MaNa slowly begins to speak again. There have been so many changes and she has witnessed so much violence in her short life. I think she will recover, but it will take time.

We have a winter garden started in the backyard. I take MaNa outside often, to feel the sun and air on her face, to help her remember our peaceful life in *TseNaCoMoCo* before we were sold into slavery. In the distance there is a forest. There is a palisade in place to protect the village from pirates, violent tribes, or other invaders. When Levi tells me this, I look at him in disbelief as I doubt Lenape would attack unprovoked.

Like his father, Levi can read my mind and simply says, "Perhaps you are right."

I have not explored the forest beyond the wall yet, but I am eager to see what herbs and roots I can find growing in the wild. I do not feel afraid but am taking time to learn as much as I can about *MaNaHahTaAn* and what is beyond our village. I am also learning to sew using cotton thread and fabric and metal needles. It is similar to the sewing of animal hides I did so long ago in *TseNaCoMoCo* using bone needles and deer tendons or finely rolled hemp.

MaNa is learning to sew, too. She is with me every minute; she will not let me out of her sight.

I am known exclusively by my English name now. I am called Rebecca Gomes. My daughter is MaNa Gomes. Levi said it would be easier for us as a family if our names were the same. I ask Levi if Mary could now be called MaNa but with his surname added. I feel it would comfort her in a deep way and help her mind and heart heal from everything that has happened.

He is so kind, he immediately says, "Of course, MaNa Gomes. What a beautiful name." Then he winks at me. Now his winking makes me blush and smile.

I have adopted the clothing style of the other Jewish women. Esther has helped me learn how to dress properly, and I keep my head covered as their religion demands. MaNa and I wear more layers, long dresses and shawls, with undergarments now instead of loincloths. MaNa and I had become familiar with the European way of dressing while living in Barbados and this is similar. Since it is already chilly, I am glad for the extra layers that add warmth.

Levi tells me there is much snow in New York and that we shall all have beaver coats by the time winter arrives. He smiles at me. His dark beard has grown fuller and longer since we have been here. Sometimes I tease him that he already has a fur coat on his face. Since the men in our tribe had very little facial hair, it takes me some time to become used to the look and feel of the thick beards the men wear, but I am accustomed to it now.

I shyly touched his beard when we began to sleep together as man and wife. I was surprised that it felt soft because it looked coarse.

I teach Levi a few PaTow'O'Mek phrases; he thinks it helps him in the shop when he is negotiating trades. My PaTow'O'Mek language is similar to the Algonquin spoken by the Lenape people here. I have asked to go to the shop to help with the business. I remind Levi that I worked for Master White and that I can interpret for him but he refuses. He tells me that Jewish women do not work outside the home in New York.

"Anyway," he says, "Soon enough you will have a baby and that will keep you busy." He smiles and winks; he is a good man. A flush of warmth flows through me now when he winks or smiles. In this short time, I have come to trust and love him. When my mind begins to think about *TseNaCoMoCo*, I push those thoughts away and instead I try to imagine what my life with Levi will be like when we are old. I hope we do have children. A sibling to help care for and nurture would help heal MaNa, too. I feel sure of it.

There is a lot to learn about life here. There are new ways of cooking with very specific rules. I am catching on quickly. Old Master Gomes is to be married soon to the recently widowed wife of the Rabbi. Levi's brother is also to be married to a neighboring widow who has two young children. He did not bring his slave wife to the New World. She and their children were sold to a plantation on the far side of Barbados. Levi says these upcoming marriages will improve the temperaments of his father and brother. I hope this is true. The new wives and children will join us in our big wooden house where we will all live together.

Old Master Gomes is stern, but he bought me from Mount Faith Manor and has given me the papers proving that MaNa and I are free. For that, I will always be grateful. He helped Levi with my escape even when he learned I had taken MaNa from the Whites and was hiding in the mikvah. He is kind underneath his gruff facade. I began to understand him a little bit better when we sailed on the *Saint Helene* for our new life.

Sailing across the ocean on the *Saint Helene* was a much different trip than being transported as slave cargo on the *Trinity*. We had hammocks for sleeping that we could put away during the day. There were curtains that divided the spaces for the various families traveling together. In our space was old Master Gomes, Levi, his two brothers: Reuben and Joseph, plus Esther, MaNa and me. MaNa and I shared a hammock. The Gomes had packed dried foods to sustain us on the trip, and there were shared barrels of water brought on board by the crew. Esther was easy to live with, quiet and efficient. I think she was grateful to have another woman to help feed and care for the men of the family. She accepted MaNa's muteness without question and would occasionally reach out and gently stroke my daughter's hair.

Esther has no children and has never been pregnant although she has been married for more than two years. She tells me she is twenty-one years old. According to the English way of calculating, I am also twenty-one. She and I are both petite; she shares her clothes and belongings with me like a sister.

She very much wants to have a baby, but her monthly bleeding lasts longer than most, sometimes up to ten days and then she is considered unclean for seven days after that. Only then is she allowed to couple with her husband, according to their religious rules. I wish I had some black cohosh and some colic root. I believe a tea made from these two plants would help with her excessive bleeding. Better yet would be if I could find *MaKaTaWai' Haw*, the Blackhaw plant, and boil the bark into tea for her. I hope to find this plant and other roots when I am finally able to explore the nearby woods. I need other healing plants for our family, but I mostly want to help Esther have a baby.

Levi and I have not officially married with any kind of ceremony, but he says we are married and refers to me as his wife. Once we arrived in the New World and were living in our house, we began to sleep together as a married couple. He has done so much for me; bought and then freed me from slavery, and accepted MaNa as his own. He is gentle, he wants to learn about my people and asks many questions about my previous life in Virginia. There is such comfort in being with him, his warmth as he holds me.

Sometimes when we lie together, he traces the outline of my snake tattoo with his finger, from my hip to my shoulder. He asks about the feathers; he wonders did it hurt when the images were applied.

I tell him, "It did not hurt, just a little prick from a crab claw."

I explain about the feathers, about their significance. "The eagle feather is the most important, as the mighty eagle is a messenger between people and the spirit world, carrying messages to O'Ki'Us and the Great Hare. A real eagle feather is white at the base and darker in the middle and at the tip."

He runs his finger over the eagle feather tattoos. There are two of them. He kisses them.

He gently touches the scar from the branded T.

I tell him, "Indeed, the burning of the T hurt very much."

He pulls me closer, hugging me and whispers, "I will protect you forever, Rebecca. I will not allow you to be hurt again."

It reminds me of the happiness I had when I was married to MaMan. It is bittersweet, as I still miss my first husband. And I miss my brother, A'KwiMex. It seems to be taking a long time to get over their deaths and that of my mother. Maybe it is because the manner of their leaving was so unexpected and violent, I do not know. I wish I could talk to Xo. She might be able to explain the grief since she lost her husband Ninj A'PaTa, suddenly and grue-somely. Her grieving was feral until her son was born and then her former spirit returned, and she smiled again.

Perhaps Levi is right, that I will soon have a baby. If I do, maybe that will help me forget the many losses. Maybe I will also drink the tea to aid in fertility. Levi, like his brothers, observes the religious tradition concerning monthly bleeding. We do not couple while I bleed, the same as my PaTow'O'Mek tradition. Additionally, Levi and I do not mate for another seven days after the bleeding has stopped, unlike my tribal practice. Esther and I are not on the same cycle, even though we have been living together since we boarded the *Saint Helene*, over three full moons ago. I think it is because something is wrong causing her excessive bleeding, but I feel it can be corrected. This is also something I wish I could discuss with Xo because her knowledge of female fertility problems far exceeds mine.

I often think of Xo and WaBus. My only longing, in terms of Barbados, is that I did not know how to get Xo and WaBus off the island, too. When Levi and I are near sleep, relaxed and warm in our bed, I have whispered their names to him. He understands, as he always does, that I miss them.

He responds to me in a kind, quiet tone, "I know, Rebecca, I know. I have not forgotten. I am still thinking about what to do." He knows how to comfort me with his words. We slumber holding hands, every night, except during my blood time and the seven days after. That small gesture makes me feel safe and protected. Often, as I listen to him breathe at night, I look at the ceiling, imagining the sky and stars beyond the roof, wondering if Xo and WaBus are even alive. I have to be content knowing that I may never know.

There is no thought given to the *Mesk YiHaKan*, seclusion in the Blood House. We just recognize the bleeding days and the associated rules and live our lives. Part of the observance for Jews means that husbands cannot touch their wives at all, in any way, during the monthly bleeding. If a husband even accidentally touches his wife, he is considered unclean and then he too must wait seven days and then take a cleansing bath. It does not make sense to me, but I do not question it.

Similarly, Levi does not understand the isolation of the *Mesk YiHaKan*. I have explained it to him, and it causes him to wonder aloud, "Who would provide the food for the men if the women were in seclusion?"

It is a valid question for our small household situation. In our PaTow'O'Mek village, not all the women were in the Blood House at the same time. Older women who no longer bled continued with the daily tribal chores, including the cooking.

I miss the time with other women, and I think Esther and I would enjoy the time together away from our responsibilities. She has asked about my tattooed skin and the scar where I am brand-ed with the letter T. I explain both to her. She tells me her religion prohibits her from marking her body. We, as PaTow'O'Mek, em-brace the embroidery, as the English call it, that the women create on one another while in the *Mesk YiHaKan*.

Esther tells me about their custom of the mikvah, the cleans-ing bath. In Barbados, she would bathe in the mikvah seven days after her bleeding ceased, to be cleansed before Yahweh and her husband. The very same mikvah where MaNa and I were hiding as we escaped! There is no mikvah in New York, so we go to the river together and dip ourselves in the frigid flowing water. It reminds me of home, but it chills Esther to the bone. It is required, nonetheless.

I have returned to the habit of daily bathing in the nearby wa-ter, and I take MaNa so she can remember our ways. The water, too, seems much colder than I remember from my days in *TseNaCoMoCo*. But it refreshes me, and I feel clean and close to my ancestors. After bathing, I look to the sky as I did so long ago and offer prayers of thanksgiving that MaNa and I are alive and safe with our new family in *MaNaHahTaAn*.

There is a slave block within walking distance of our house and the shop, but closer to the wall. It horrifies me to see the African slaves: chained, naked, shorn and oiled, prepared for sale. I know what it feels like to be treated as less than human. I still have a fear that this could happen to me again, even though I have papers stating I am free. I have not seen an Indigenous person on the slave block thus far, but I know it is possible. It has happened before.

This is another thing I whisper to Levi in the privacy of our bed, deep in the night. I tell him I am afraid I will be captured and sold again.

I tell him, "I wish we could move to Virginia."

"Rebecca, shhhh, go to sleep. There are slave blocks in Virginia, too, even more than in *MaNaHahTaAn*."

He is right. I can never forget that it was in Virginia where I and the other women and children were captured and sold. The safest place to be is in New York with Levi and his family, so I settle into this life with gratitude.

Even with the thankfulness, I still think of my ancestors and the PaTow'O'Mek, and wonder if anyone survived the massacre and if there is a remnant of the tribe left. If so, where are they living? How are they doing? I feel at peace about it though, living near the ShaTeMuc River with Levi and his family and MaNa. This life is so different, sometimes I feel I have lived three separate lives: my early years with my tribe in *TseNaCoMoCo*, the years in Barbados and now with my husband and MaNa in New York. I am content to be here, free and living in peace.

Eventually, I explore beyond the palisade. I forage in the nearby woods for herbs and roots. I see the local tribal people and I greet them saying, "*WinGaPo*" and they answer me with the same words. I can tell they are perplexed that although I speak Algonquin, my attire is different. I am wearing a long dress, an apron, a cape, a shawl that covers my head and leather shoes, apparel made of cloth and wool that is foreign to them. Some of these Lenape have a piece or two of European clothing, acquired while trading, but mostly they wear the traditional fur mantles and tunics, leather leggings and moccasins.

After I have seen them several times, I ask if they know of the PaTow'O'Mek tribe who live in Virginia. They confirm that yes, they do know of this tribe. They tell me the village was destroyed many moons ago by the colonial government in order to take the land. I do not reveal that I am PaTow'O'Mek. I just nod, indicating I have heard and understood their words.

A stillness settles over my spirit. I look to the sky for the Great Hare but I do not see Him, so then I say a prayer to Jesus thanking Him for saving MaNa. I pray again, this time to Yahweh, thanking Him for Levi and our survival through so many difficult days.

Xo
(Shining Moon)/Leah

WINTER, 1670

TSENACOMOCO, VIRGINIA

*I*t is smokey and dark in the Mesk YiHaKan. I can barely recognize *the faces of the women who are sharing the space with me. A sudden strong wind blows open the door mat and the smoldering fire flares up brightly. Now I can see that the Blood House is filled with my deceased ancestors and other dead tribe members. I can tell they are spirits, but they appear as human and they begin to chant in unison, "It is time, NePa'WeXo, it is time."*

Then the chorus becomes jumbled and with outstretched hands, they call to me, "It is your time, Xo, it is your time, come with us." Then one by one the specters float up to the ceiling and out through the smoke hole. When there is one spirit left, she takes me by the hand trying to pull me along but before I go through the opening I say, "MaTa, No! It is not my time." I struggle to escape her grip and when I am successful, I fall heavily back to the floor, landing with a thud.

I am, in fact, in the *Mesk YiHaKan,* the Blood House. There are no apparitions, just the dying embers and the slumbering bodies of the other women. I stand quietly and add a few pieces of wood to the fire. A shiver goes through me. It is cold and the dream has disturbed my sleep. I wrap a large bearskin around my body and lie back down, thinking about all that has happened.

* * *

I had been hiding among the barrels of sugar and rum for less than a day when I heard the yelling of the deckhands followed by the rocking of the *Mermaid* as the ship pulled away from the dock and set sail for Virginia. I remember being suddenly overcome with fear that perhaps WaBus and the Lewises were not on the flying boat, but what could I do now? At that point my fate was sealed. It was dark and dank in my hiding place. I ate a few bites of the dried meat, rationalizing the need to stay strong. I convinced myself I would find something to eat eventually, even if I had to resort to killing one of the ever-present rats that huddled nearby. It would not be the first time I had eaten rat to survive.

The next day, I was dozing when I heard footsteps and whispers that sounded like "*WinGaPo?*"

I made a low whistle using my fingers and listened.

The whistle was repeated back, and I knew my dear WaBus was looking for me and was, indeed, on the ship. I crept toward the sound of her whistle, and she came to mine, and we hugged with great enthusiasm that threatened to topple us over between the cargo. I pulled her by the hand to my hiding place, and we giggled like children. There were no words for our happiness. She pulled a piece of bread from her pocket and handed it to me.

"Now that I know you are here, I will bring you more food," she said, smiling. "I cannot linger, I do not want to make anyone suspicious." As she started to leave, we embraced once more and she said quietly "*NihTe KihTe*" one hand to her heart and the other to the sky, and then she was gone. Yes, our hearts would always be bound together.

I knew I could tolerate anything now. My daughter was on the ship, and we were heading to *TseNaCoMoCo*. After all that we had endured, I was on my way to finding my son and holding him in my arms once more. I had no doubt that I would find him.

I never knew when to expect my daughter, but she would appear at least once a day with a morsel of bread, a sliver of dried meat or a piece of sugar candy. I dozed and dreamed, trying to formulate an escape plan for when we landed in Virginia. I could not decide on a course of action. I hoped the way out would be made clear upon arrival. I was living in a state of suspension, but I knew I could endure it because freedom was near. We were never able to talk for long as my WaBus was busy almost every minute taking care of the Lewis children. Thankfully, it did not seem that Master Lewis had tried to harm her in any way yet, so I felt peaceful about our ocean passage thus far. I still reminded her to stay out of his way, that he was wicked and unpredictable.

We had been at sea for perhaps fourteen days and nights when the ocean started getting rough, and the *Mermaid* began rocking ferociously, causing some of the cargo to break loose from the ropes that secured them. The barrels whirled around, battering each other, creaking, and threatening to break open. It was dangerous, and I struggled to keep my balance and stay clear of the rolling cargo. The belly of the *Mermaid* began to take on water, and it sloshed around with the movement of the ship. I tried to stay dry and hold still in a higher spot, but the wood became slippery when it got wet and then I, too, became drenched. As I did when vicious weather came to the Potomac River, I prayed to O'Ki'Us to calm the waters and to guide the ship safely to shore as soon as possible.

As I finished my prayer there was a terrible crash and the ship seemed destined to sink. I found out later that lightning had struck one of the masts, and it had cracked in half. The crew worked furiously to free the ship of the waterlogged sail and splintered wood that was attempting to drag the whole vessel down to a watery grave at the bottom of the sea. I do not know how many hours the *Mermaid* bobbed and struggled to stay afloat, but at last the winds abated and there was an eerie silence.

The quiet spell was broken by WaBus bounding down into the hold calling loudly for me. "*Nek*! Mother!"

"What? Shhhhh!" I answered. "Are you injured?"

"It's Master Lewis. He was struck by the falling sail. His lower leg is broken, open to the air. He is still bleeding. Mother, you have to help him. There is no one else on the ship who knows how to heal or fix bones."

"I cannot, WaBus, I will be thrown overboard for being a stowaway. It is too dangerous," I could not imagine in that moment caring for and healing the one who had been my tormentor for the past almost four years. I had wished him dead so many times. I stared at my daughter in disbelief. Did she not know me at all?

Ultimately, I followed my WaBus up the ladder and revealed my presence not only to Master Lewis but to the Captain and crew as well. There were several injuries; cuts and broken arms. One sailor was missing after being swept overboard and lost to the elements during the storm. Because of the damage to the ship and injured passengers, the fact that I was a stowaway was overlooked, at least for the moment.

Master Lewis was lying upon a table in a room near the galley, moaning in pain, his leg in a pool of blood that was dripping onto the floor. My mind immediately went back to the *Trinity* when I nursed Elizabeth back to life.

When he saw me, he said, "Leah, help me" as if he had never treated me cruelly or abused me. As if he did not remember that just days ago he had tried to leave me behind in Barbados while he took my daughter away to serve as his slave in the New World. His bullying and meanness stripped away, replaced with helplessness and begging.

But this I saw as his inherent belief that he deserved anything he desired, and now he wished to be helped even though he had maliciously refused to help those who had been dependent on him all those years in Barbados.

I hated him even more. I realized in that moment that if I had slit his throat as I had fantasized so many times, he would not have bellowed but would have whimpered as he lay dying.

With so many eyes upon me, I called for sugar wine and looked at the bottled herbs. Once he was drunk, the sailors in the room held him down and I attempted to pull the bones into alignment, to set them in the proper position to heal. He screamed from the pain and passed out. I then washed the injury with water, followed by a rinsing with sugar wine and again with water. Using a board to stabilize the bones, I wrapped his leg in linen strips.

I had a sinking feeling in my gut because usually this type of break results in death if the open area becomes swollen, red and seeps pus. If that happens, the leg must be amputated. I knew the English used amputation more than we did in our tribe; there were limited options at this point on the *Mermaid*. I hoped we would arrive at the port before his leg became infected in that way.

I had seen a one-legged man in Bridgetown at church and had heard slaves talking about his survival. And there were many slaves on the sugar plantations whose hands or fingers, even arms had been cut off after being caught in the sugar cane press. Amputation was not something we practiced in our tribe in *TseNaCoMoCo*, and I had never had to perform such an act. I did not know how Master Lewis would heal or even if he would heal. His ultimate fate would be decided another day.

To keep from being thrown overboard as a stowaway, I then treated the crew's injuries. Most of them were minor, and I made poultices with the herbs from the galley and medicine room, mixed with olive oil. I cleaned and wrapped the wounds. I pulled the two broken arms into place and bound them. The captain told me to stay in the sick room with the injured and nurse them to wellness. I knew there were no guarantees, even though my life depended on it. The journey continued with the *Mermaid* limping along, one sail short.

The days passed and land finally appeared on the horizon. As I watched, I realized we were docking at Point Comfort—the same place we had boarded the *Trinity* so many moons ago when we left *TseNaCoMoCo*. There was no jubilant cheer this time, just a general feeling that everyone wanted to get off the *Mermaid* as quickly as possible. I stayed near WaBus and the wet nurse, trying to look like I belonged to the Lewis assembly. Mistress Lewis would have been the only person to object, but because of her husband's injuries, she now had to make decisions and was distracted by the weight her choices.

Even trying to get the family off the ship proved difficult. Mistress Lewis looked scared and unsure, but I knew she would find the strength to navigate this unexpected circumstance. I just hoped it would not include having me killed.

Master Lewis's brother arrived with two carriages to collect the family, trunks and slaves who were in tow, including me. Master Lewis was not well; his leg was not healing and he was in tremendous pain. When we arrived at his brother's house, I knew we would need to leave immediately. We were taken to the slave quarters while the Lewises were getting settled in the main house. The advantage would be ours if we disappeared quickly, so WaBus and I left in the middle of that first night.

I knew where I was. I knew the stars. I knew we needed to head north to get to our homeland on the shores of the Potomac River.

We journeyed through the woods, foraging for edible plants and nuts. I had not forgotten anything and, for the first time in so many years, I felt hopeful about the future, confident about finding my son and living in peace with however many of the tribe remained. Surely, some PaTow'O'Mek were still alive? I shuddered at the thought that perhaps any living tribe members had been hunted down and killed. Why had I not considered that before? I wondered if any other women had returned from Barbados.

We were careful to avoid detection as we traveled north. While I doubted the Lewis family would immediately look for WaBus and me, I did not want to count on it. So we made ourselves as inconspicuous as possible, scrounging for sustenance that grew freely from the earth and from planted gardens we found along the way. I knew some of the southern Virginia tribes. We had traded woven eel traps, dogs, and antimony with them. It was not unusual for the Nansemond or Pamunkey tribes to travel north for days to trade with the PaTow'O'Mek for these things. Our tribes had enjoyed a good relationship and had been friendly, but that was many moons ago. I did not think it would be safe to expect protection from the Nansemond without knowing their current allegiances. They were in such close proximity to Point Comfort.

So we did not seek them out, and kept walking. We had no way of knowing what had happened in the years we had been gone. I wanted to discuss this with WaBus, but she was too young when we left to understand the shifting coalitions between the various tribes and the colonial invaders. She did have a highly developed intuition, probably honed by surviving the massacre and the subsequent time as a slave in Barbados. It was her keen eye that first noticed signs of a nearby settlement after six days of walking.

I realized we were near the Pamunkey tribe who lived along the Pamunkey River, north of the Nansemond but south of the PaTow'O'Mek tribal land. The Pamunkey were a larger tribe than we were, very influential in *TseNaCoMoCo* because the famous paramount Chief Powhatan had been a Pamunkey. Our tribes had intermarried and traded. I was suddenly filled with exhilaration, being this close to home. I could feel my spirit soar as we saw deer and fox, animals we had not seen in Barbados.

The walnut trees, the marshes and waterways seemed to whisper to me, "You are home."

I fought the urge to grab WaBus by the hand and run through the woods straight into the settlement. Instead, I clung to our tribal culture of restraint, knowing that caution and careful consideration would get us safely to the Potomac.

From what we deemed a safe distance and hidden by the lush growth of the trees during early *NePiNough,* the Time of Harvesting, we watched the Pamunkey return to their village after a day of foraging and gathering wood. We were so entranced watching that we did not hear approaching footsteps until a group was upon us and we were surrounded. Four scowling Pamunkey men, dressed in traditional clothing with the right sides of their heads shaved and the left side hair braided or bound into a knot, held their bows in hand. I could see their quivers, arrows and other tools strapped to their bodies.

I could not maintain my calm demeanor and I broke out into a big smile and started laughing. WaBus kept a straight face, fearing I had at last lost my mind. It was pure joy that made me smile and laugh and within minutes, my eyes were overflowing with tears as I continued to laugh and cry uncontrollably. Maybe I had gone mad, my mind turned to mush with happiness to be near home, among my people.

Between the sobs, I tried to say, "I am Xo, I am PaTow'O'Mek."

The men looked to one another and then back to me and finally to WaBus. My thoughts and words were jumbled but when they understood that we had lived through the massacre of the tribe and were returning home, all four of the men smiled and embraced my daughter and me. We walked toward their village together.

That night the Pamunkey women cooked a feast to celebrate our survival and return. I told the story of our survival: of how the men in our tribe had been killed in cold blood, how the women had been marched to Point Comfort, how my baby son had been stolen, of our terrible journey on the *Trinity*, how we had been sold into slavery in Barbados and of our escape.

We danced and smoked in celebration but I, too, had questions for them.

Had any of the PaTow'O'Mek survived the massacre? The answer was "*MaTa*, No." Every man in the village was killed and the women and children taken away. But there were PaTow'O'Mek men who had been working on colonial farms at the time who had not been slaughtered.

What about the stolen babies? Had there been rumors about the Strangers raising native babies around the time of the massacre?

"*BiCi*, yes." There had been some chatter about native babies, particularly a young boy with green eyes.

My heart was suddenly in my throat. It had to be my son, my ToWawh Nu'KwiSus, my Strong Son. His green eyes unusual in our tribe but not in our family because of the rape of my mother by the Spanish priest so long ago.

"Do you know where he is?" I tried to remain calm, but my knees grew wobbly with the thought of being reunited. I would steal him back from whatever family had raised him. My resolve steadied my shaky knees, but I could not slow my pounding heart.

"He is not with a colonial family; he is with the Portobacco," came the answer.

My mind raced with a thousand other questions, but I dared not ask them. I did not want to take the time to ask them. I wanted to leave immediately. I wanted to claim my son. I tried to still my racing heart with deep breaths as I sat and listened.

The story continued to unfold.

After our tribe had been destroyed, the colonial government also killed many of the Portobacco tribe, although not the complete annihilation the PaTaw'O'Mek had experienced. Other tribes suffered losses as well in the summer of 1666. There had been a wholesale effort to remove the tribes along the Potomac and Rappahannock Rivers. The remnant populations of the different tribes joined together for survival, leaving the sacred lands upon which they had always farmed and foraged. In order to survive, they were forced to become more nomadic and secretive to evade the wrath of the English.

WaBus and I stayed there with the Pamunkey tribe for two days: eating, resting and regaining our strength. They were gracious, and the time there restored my being and gave me hope for an abundant life with my daughter and son. We were invited to stay and live with the tribe, but they understood the desire of my heart to be reunited with my missing child and possibly even find the brother I had barely known and hardly remembered. When it was time for us to continue our journey north, three Pamunkey men joined us as escorts and we left via canoe, this time on the Mattaponi River toward what was left of the Portobacco tribe.

The peaceful lapping of the water on the canoe as it skimmed the surface reminded me of my childhood. My mind was flooded with the pleasant images of my mother, my friend Ah'SaWei, her daughter MaNa and her mother. I closed my eyes and turned my face toward the sky.

WaBus and I were almost home.

* * *

As I REMEMBER THESE HAPPENINGS, the sun is beginning to rise and the other women in the *Mesk YiHaKan* are stirring. This is not my first sleepless night in *TseNaCoMoCo*, but I would rather have a sleepless night here with my people than sleep soundly anywhere else in the world. I smile to myself and snuggle next to WaBus, who is now a woman, spending her bleeding days with me and the other women in the seclusion and comfort of the *Mesk YiHaKan*.

Ah'SaWei
(Golden Fawn)/Rebecca

I thought I knew what complete heartbreak felt like after my husband and brother were murdered on that hot summer night in 1666, but I was wrong. I thought the way my chest would tighten as if bound by a rope, the constriction that would move to my throat, my tears choking out my breath, forcing me to gasp for air, was the worst anguish I would ever know, but I was wrong. The way I could not speak, my tongue and mouth thick with despair and longing for my husband and, yes, my brother, too. And the numb emptiness that came when my mother died after her first day in the sugar fields of Barbados. I had survived the wretchedness of grief back then only because I wanted to be with my daughter. I was kept alive by the thinnest strand of hope, that of being with my child, MaNa. I did not want my daughter to be alone.

The sorrow never totally went away.

The viciousness of the losses, followed by the extended horror and death I saw on the *Trinity* and in Barbados, forced me to live with a harsher reality than I thought possible. Sometimes, unexpectedly, I would see my brother in my mind, returning from his *HusKaNaw*, laughing, with the snake in his earlobe. Or Levi might gently press his forehead to mine with affection, and I would think of my dead husband, MaMan. They were never completely gone from me. But over time there was happiness again.

As fall turns to winter, I often leave the protection of the wall and venture further into the nearby forest. I am not afraid. The local Lenape are used to seeing MaNa and me foraging in the forest, collecting herbs, wild onions, berries, nuts and a variety of healing plants that grew in the loamy soil. Occasionally, Esther joins us, but she is never entirely comfortable getting too far from the house we share with the extended Gomes family.

I finally find the shrub with the red tinged, glossy green leaves, the one we call *MaKaTaWai' Haw*, Blackhaw, that we used to help ease the monthly bleeding and minimize the cramping that some women experienced. I cut several thick stems from the bottom of the bush where the bark was hardier and take them back to our house.

I show the cuttings to Esther and tell her, "We will boil the bark into tea, Esther. I think this will solve your bleeding problem so you can have a baby."

I have her drink a small amount every day and, after just two moon cycles, her bleeding days are now the typical five days instead of ten. She becomes pregnant the following month, early in *PoPaNaw*, winter. Esther is elated to finally be with child. She tells me stories from the Bible about women who had waited many years before Yahweh filled their wombs with life. She tells me the stories of Sarah and of Rachel. She is so happy, as is Reuben, her husband. Old Master Gomes smiles more than usual; he cannot help himself.

Esther's pregnancy lends an air of hopeful anticipation to the Gomes household. The addition of the new wives for old Master Gomes and his remaining bachelor son, Joseph, has been straightforward, and the women seem quietly pleased about a new baby. As the wife of old Master Gomes, the former Rabbi's wife attempts to take charge of the household. She enjoys telling everyone what to do, bossing the other women around, criticizing the cleaning or the cooking.

If Master Gomes hears her, he just calmly says, "Wife, enough."

She then settles down at least for a moment. Her only child with the Rabbi died as an infant. She is now past the age to have a baby. Even with her bossiness, she pats Esther's belly when she passes her in the kitchen.

The young girl and boy who joined our household through marriage are rambunctious, and it takes a few weeks for MaNa to warm to their presence. My daughter is still quiet, more so than most children. In time they accept and include her in their playing. They are both older than MaNa, so they often treat her as a baby, or try to trick her into eating or drinking something sour or unpleasant, but in a familial way. It began to feel comfortable like a family should feel, much like the contentment I had experienced growing up in my tribe so many moons ago.

After Esther's success, I begin to drink the Blackhaw tea as well. I do not seem to have any obvious problems with my moon cycle. Yet I have not become pregnant, even though Levi and I couple frequently, after the time of abstinence and bathing required by his religion. When we are abstaining and not touching during my unclean days, Levi catches my eye and winks if he passes through the kitchen.

On the first night after the nights of abstinence and bathing, he whispers, "Rebecca, Ah'SaWei, Rebecca, Ah'SaWei," and then laughs gently as he nuzzles my neck, tickling me with his beard. He teases me and says if we have a son, he would be born with a full beard. I can tell Levi likes to make me smile and sometimes he is so silly, I laugh out loud.

Around the beginning of *CaTaPeuk*, early spring, old Master Gomes suddenly begins to feel sick with fever and develops a terrible ache in his head. He feels so unwell; he has to take to his bed. His wife tries to care for him, but she has an ominous feeling that he will not survive, and she will be widowed again.

Her fear paralyzes her, so Esther and I take over the nursing duties, trying to help him take small swallows of water and drink a tea that would induce vomiting, to get rid of the illness. Over the coming days, he develops lesions in his mouth and on his tongue. He refuses to ingest any more liquids. The illness is slow in developing, but eventually his face is covered with red, hard blisters that spread to his chest, arms, legs, feet and hands. He is delirious with fever, and it appears he will die.

Although old Master Gomes is the first in our household to become sick with the disease that was called smallpox, he does not die. As he lies near death, though, others in the house became sick, one by one.

Old Master Gomes' wife survives because she leaves the house. I never knew where she went exactly. One day just after Esther and I have taken over the care of her husband, she packs a small bag and leaves. All she says as she stands in the doorway is, "I'm sorry."

She is close to many people in the Jewish community from her previous station as the Rabbi's wife and I assume she called upon some of those relationships. The rest of us, even the children, contract smallpox. It is a time of great suffering in our family. The disease ravages our household.

Esther dies first, before ever giving birth. She never held her child in her arms. Her husband, Reuben, succumbs after she dies.

When Levi starts to feel unwell, he tries to pretend it is not true. But when the hard blisters come, he knows. He won't let me in the room, he doesn't want me to get sick. I go in to care for him anyway, once he is too weak to order me to leave. As he is dying, I hold his hand. He no longer responds and as he leaves this life, a tear makes a trail down the side of his head.

I drop my head onto his chest and remember when Master White had prayed to Jesus for MaNa to be healed. I try to remember the words.

"Jesus, heal my husband as you did MaNa so long ago. Please hear this prayer." I am desperate for him to live. Then I remember the Whites had been on their knees, so I get on my knees and pray again.

I wait for him to revive and say, "I'm thirsty," but he doesn't move. Old Master Gomes is still too sick; he cannot speak with Yahweh. I try to reach Yahweh by lifting my hands but nothing. As a last resort, I force myself away from my husband and go outside. Looking to the sky, I search for the Great Hare, but again, nothing.

All three children get sick, even MaNa. They die within a day of each other. Yes, death comes for my beautiful MaNa, my butterfly, my Mary. This hollows me out, too empty to feel any more pain. This is when I know a deeper anguish than ever before.

I develop the telltale fever after everyone else has been sick. The throbbing pain in my skull finally forces me to lie down, and I curl beside my dear MaNa. Her face is disfigured from all the sores, but she is still lovely. Her little body is covered with bruising from the many bleeding, oozing pox. I have not been able to coax her into drinking any water. I resort to wetting a piece of cloth and squeeze small droplets onto her chapped and peeling lips. It is a pitiful sight, and I am numb, unbelieving our end would come this way.

Levi has been in the ground for two days when I hold my dying daughter. As she takes her last breath, she seems to reach for someone or something, perhaps my mother calling to her, maybe her father waiting to help her with the passage.

I do not cry. I have no tears left. There is nothing left. I just hold her and close my eyes as I wait for death to take me next. I do not want to linger any longer. There is no reason to live.

I fall asleep and eventually awake clinging to the body of my dead child. She looks peaceful even though covered with the pox. Old Master Gomes arranges for her to be buried next to Levi and the others. He is weak after the long ordeal and his face is scarred from the lesions. Even though frail, he insists on mourning in the Jewish tradition that involves seven days of observance of the loss.

I cannot understand how he is counting as so many had died within days of each other. When his wife hears he has recovered, she returns to our house.

Over the coming weeks, I can tell I am slowly getting better, and that death has mocked me by refusing to take me, when I wanted so desperately to join my daughter, Levi and my other ancestors. I am angry and hopeless.

I do not want to live without MaNa.

I can tell from the reaction of others when they look upon me that my face is disfigured and scarred from the damage the sores had left behind, but I do not care. I look at my reflection in the water one morning as I bathe. I do not recognize the deformed and bereft woman staring back at me. I find a shell, sharpen it on a nearby rock and cut off my hair. The mourning ritual of my people does nothing to ease the pain.

As spring, the Time of Fish Runs, is quickly becoming the Time for Planting and Growing, I know I can no longer stay in New York. I now yearn for *TseNaCoMoCo* and, without MaNa or Levi, I have nothing to keep me in this place. I know I need to tell old Master Gomes, but I do not know how he will respond. He is still somewhat unsteady, but he has started going back to the shop for a few hours a day to help with the sorting and shipping of fur.

I call to him as he opens the door to leave one morning.

"Yes, Rebecca." He turns to face me and leans heavily on the cane he has been using as he recovers. His scarred face looks tired, his beard is completely white now, but there is kindness in his eyes. I realize how much I have come to love him as I look into his sorrowful eyes.

There is no easy way to say it, so I just blurt out the words. "I have to go home; I have to go to Virginia and see if any of my people are still alive." As I say the words, my voice falters and I might cry.

"Oh, Rebecca, your home is here now. You are a part of us even though Levi is gone and even though our, your MaNa—dear MaNa is in the ground as well." He hesitates. "I consider you as my daughter; you have been loyal and true. I will always be grateful for the tender care you provided when I was so sick. Think about this for a few days, Rebecca. Do not make this decision hastily, while still mired in grief."

He nods to me and turns to walk to work. He is a man of few words, but those words mean so much to me.

While I am touched and surprised, his words do not change my heart. I need to head south; I need to leave soon while the weather is mild and traveling easier.

Master Gomes arranges for two of the local Lenape to travel with me as far as Virginia. The men have occasionally worked as guides for European explorers and are familiar with the terrain. We take three Big Dogs that make the journey much easier and faster than walking. The men are instructed to trade for fur along the way back.

Master Gomes repeats these words to me many times before I leave. "Rebecca, if your people are not there when you get to Virginia, come back to us. You are always welcome here." He repeats this to the guides as well, that they should bring me back safely to New York if I do not find what I am looking for.

Despite Master Gomes's kindness and urging me to stay, I know I need to try and find what is left of the PaTow'O'Mek tribe. While I feel anxious anticipation, I have no second thoughts about leaving.

After being near death, ravaged by the smallpox infection and heavy of heart with the losses of my husband and daughter, and even longing for death, I now feel something different. I realized my will to live has returned. The scabs have fallen off of my face and body. The sun feels warm on the tender new pock-scarred skin. The soft spring breeze gently lifts the new growth of my hair. It is a sunny day in late spring when I leave New York. The bright green tips on the plants seem to guide the way south, lighting the path forward.

My Lenape companions and I do not say much as we travel. We have enough of the Algonquin language in common to communicate when necessary. Being Indigenous, they understand completely the connection to the earth and to one's tribe. They know my story of survival from the massacre to being sold and living as a slave. They know of the unspeakable loss of family that has occurred, in losing both of my husbands, my birth family and my child. Every tribe along the East Coast of the New World has experienced similar losses. There are no words to describe the devastation. We do not need words as we travel to *TseNaCoMoCo*.

We travel light. I have my beaver coat, the one given to me by Levi. I roll and bind it by day and use it as a sleeping mat and blanket at night. Inside the folds it holds a few pieces of clothing and a dress that had been MaNa's before she got sick. Within the first day, I shed my headscarf and outer shawl, placing them within the bundle strapped to my horse. We eat dried venison we brought along and forage for greens and onions, cooking them for the evening meal. Along the way, we stop at two trading stations, at each one asking about news or survivors from the PaTow'O'Mek tribe.

My heart skips a beat, or so it seems, when we were told that the surviving PaTow'O'Mek are living with the remaining Portobacco tribe. We learn that many Portobacco were killed in the months after my tribe was destroyed. The English even killed the chief they had appointed, Chief ToDoNoBo WeSKin. Poor Chief Milk Eye had not been spared. I show no outward emotion as we hear this news, a small nod to acknowledge only that I understand what has been said.

As we get closer to *TseNaCoMoCo*, I remembered that last encounter with the Portobacco. How we had been rebuffed and how angry A'KwiMex had become. But then I am flooded with warmth remembering that just before that, we had been collecting tuckahoe with our mother on the river and how peaceful our lives had been. I hope for that life again, but I know everything will be different, now that so many Strangers have come to the our land.

The guides send word to alert the Portobacco of our visit. As we near their camp, I am eager and yet scared of what I might find. It is late afternoon, and the sun is shining in golden beams that are almost blinding from our position on the Big Dogs.

I put one hand to my forehead as a shield so I can see and with the other, I cradle my rounded belly. I have concealed my secret thus far; I am pregnant with Levi's baby.

WaBus

(Blue Bunny)/Anne

It is the plentiful time of year, late in *NePiNough*, the Time of Harvesting, when most of the crops have been gathered and there are plenty of fresh vegetables and corn to eat. We ate a feast tonight in celebration of the bounty, and we now sit around the fire, listening to the music of the drums. I am relaxed as my newborn nurses at my breast; my two-year-old is playing nearby with my brother who is now six years old. Yes! My brother, ToWawh Nu'KwiSus, Strong Son, was found, living with the Portobacco tribe on the north shore of the Potomac River. Let me go back— let me try to explain all that has happened.

* * *

MY MOTHER, XO, IS BRAVER THAN ANYONE I know: man, woman, or even the strongest beast. I confess, there were times I did not believe we would find our way back to *TseNaCoMoCo*. There were so many obstacles. Death faced us constantly from the time we were marched away from our burned village, as we boarded the *Trinity*, while we lived as slaves in Barbados, and then still when we returned to our homeland. I was a child. I did not completely understand how dangerous it was; I just knew my mother would keep me safe. She taught me everything I know about life and survival. She showed me how to care for women in childbirth and how to find plants to heal injury and illness. She taught me to trust my instincts and that knowledge has kept me alive. I am now following in her footsteps to help the women in the tribe with childbirth and fertility.

My mother is sitting on the opposite side of the circle this evening, holding her infant daughter. Her eyes are closed, but she is smiling as she sways gently to the beat of the drums, rocking her child to sleep. Her hair has strands of silver now. Her eyes still sparkle with flecks of green, the color has not faded with age. She thought she was too old to have another baby when she married again. This baby was an unexpected delight after so much heartache. She relishes every detail of this infant girl. She has found peace being married and settled, once again, in *TseNaCoMoCo*.

Being reunited with her son restored her soul, gave her new light and energy. She, who had been so hurt and abused, who had considered murdering another human being, was now content. Beside her sits her lifelong best friend, Ah'SaWei. They sway in unison, the movement slight, but definitely there. Here we are, more than six years after our tribe was massacred, the only three women who returned. We have not given up hope, though. Perhaps others will show up, and we will rejoice that they too have survived.

I learned a lot while living in Barbados, as a slave with the Lewis family. I was a child in charge of children. Children universally like to play, and they respond well to kindness, so overseeing the Lewis children was easy for me. I had cared for my baby brother and other tribal children before we were captured, so I knew what to do. I learned the ways of the English because I was invisible to them, just a piece of property in the room. I could observe their habits, their quirks, their petty grievances.

In the midst of it, I learned to speak, write and count in English. Now that we are back in Virginia, being fluent in both PaTow'O'Mek and English has been hugely beneficial. I have been able to interpret when the Strangers show up with demands or wanting to trade. It is much harder for them to cheat us now that some of us know their language.

I learned to survive. I instinctively knew to stay out of the way when Mistress Lewis was on a rampage. She was loud and emotional and would break objects in anger. I did not blame her. She was just out of childhood herself and married to a tyrant. Staying away from Master Lewis was a bit trickier but I was mostly able to avoid him. He was known to rape his slave women. He savagely beat the men. My mother warned me within days of our arrival at Sugar Grove Plantation to never be caught alone in a room with him. There were a few times he tried to grab me, but I twisted myself out of his grasp and ran away. He was usually so drunk that he was unable to catch me. He did not forget those attempts.

When we boarded the *Mermaid* for the journey to the New World, I was surprised to see that the wet nurse and I would have hammocks just on the other side of a curtain, across from the Lewis family. I do not know what I imagined before we boarded; the only other time I had been on a ship was as cargo, stored beneath the upper decks. Other families and individuals were traveling on the *Mermaid*. We heard all the bickering, the crying, the vomiting from seasickness; there was no privacy. I stayed busy emptying the family chamber pot and trying to entertain the children. The wet nurse ended up mostly caring for and feeding the baby.

Early one morning, before the sun came up, Master Lewis grabbed me from my hammock while I was sleeping and, with his hand over my mouth, walked me toward the ladder that went to the deck below. This was where all the supplies were held, and barrels of rum were stored, all of which would be sold once we arrived at port. Unbeknownst to him, this was also where my mother was hiding as a stowaway.

He was not drunk, and he was strong. He did not try to hide what he had planned, and although we were on the lower deck, we were in plain sight if anyone should pass by. He did not care.

He growled in my ear, "Did you think I had forgotten all the times you weaseled your way out of my grip? Did you think I would never have you, as I have had your mother and every other slave woman I have owned? Did you, Anne? If you did, you gravely miscalculated."

I understood his intentions, and I knew he was determined. I had never been with a man; I had not had my first blood yet although my mother said she was sure it would come soon. My thoughts were racing as I tried to think of how to get away. As he had awakened me from sleep, my bladder was full and I wondered if I released the contents on him would he stop the assault? Would it make him angrier? Before I could go any further with that thought, he roughly grabbed my crotch, inserting his hand inside my undergarment and tried to tear it off. He suddenly withdrew his hand and held it to the light. It was covered in blood.

"You filthy little witch! I didn't know you were bleeding! Your dirt is all over me now." He shoved me such that I fell to the floor and slid a few feet away from him. He looked disgusted and he spat at me, but he missed.

He then said, "I'll keep track of your days, don't worry. I will have you, that I promise." He climbed back up the ladder, leaving me there.

I was trembling, but I had to smile. My first moon blood had come at the perfect time to prevent my being raped. I knew that our tribe did not mate during the bleeding time, but not because women were considered dirty. I had heard that the English and other Europeans thought women were unclean and dangerous while bleeding, but never did I think my moon blood would save me from being attacked. I sat up and straightened my clothes. I wanted to run to my mother and tell her everything, but I was afraid she would reveal herself and kill him in front of everyone, thus ensuring her own death. His cruelty had pushed her to the point of near insanity.

So I kept this secret to myself.

It was about ten days later that we started to feel the storm coming. The sea was getting rougher, and the wind was blowing. I was with the children trying to distract them so they would not be scared when Master Lewis approached. He demanded I accompany him and escorted me by the arm, pulling me again toward the ladder to go below. The ship lurched suddenly, and I jerked my arm from his grip and scampered instead up the ladder to the open deck. He followed, bellowing for me to come back. The deck was slippery with water, and the waves were washing over the sides. I grabbed onto the nearest rope to keep from being washed overboard. The next thing I saw was the sky open up bright white and the biggest, loudest bolt of lightning I had ever seen came directly toward the ship and struck one of the masts, cracking it and briefly catching the wood on fire.

The storm was raging loudly, the sailors trying frantically to keep the ship from sinking as the sail dragged through the ocean. I had to get below to safety. I needed to get down off the deck. Then I saw him. Master Lewis had been hit by the falling mast and lay with his leg broken, open to the elements. A large piece of wood lay on his chest immobilizing him.

At this point, the people were in charge of their own survival. It appeared we would all be lost at sea and likely drowned. I carefully made my way to the hatch, passing by Master Lewis.

As I tried to slip by him, our eyes met and he said, "Help me, Anne."

Help him? His arrogance was unbelievable, after all the suffering he had caused my mother and me and countless others. I walked by him and started down the ladder. Then the thought came to me: Did I want to be like him? Did I want to be ruthless and let him die? Leave his children fatherless as other barbarians had left me fatherless?

I hesitated another minute and then went to his side and tried to move the broken piece of timber off his chest. His leg was bleeding heavily or maybe it was just the rain making it look like a lot. I knew it was a serious break and his life was in danger. A sailor helped me drag him to the hatch and we pulled him to safety, taking him to a room near the galley. All the movement and pain had caused him to briefly pass out. The sailor and I looked at each other and I knew what I had to do. I ran to get my mother; she was the only person who could help with this disaster.

After her initial resistance, she revealed herself not just as a stowaway but also as a valuable healer with skills to save lives by setting broken bones and mixing soothing poultices. She kept Master Lewis alive till we landed at Point Comfort. The port looked very much the same as it had when we left, though there were more ships and more structures on land. My mother told me she remembered everything; she knew how to get us home. I trusted her completely and we disappeared into the dark night within hours of being shown the slave quarters.

As we walked north, she pointed out edible plants that we ate with gratitude. Wild blackberries still grew on the vines, ripe for eating. We plucked a few baby squash from planted gardens and ate them raw, they were so tender at that stage. We encountered Indigenous folks along the way whom we cautiously observed. We spent two nights with the Pamunkey tribe who told us the few surviving PaTow'O'Mek men were now living with the Portobacco tribe. We continued our journey north.

The events when we walked into the Portobacco camp will be seared into my mind for eternity. Runners had been sent ahead to announce our arrival. As we entered the village, the people cheered and clapped for us. Men and women that my mother hardly knew ran to her, embracing her, many with tears in their eyes.

After the happy exaltations quieted, my mother tried to speak but all she could do was whisper, her voice was so filled with emotion.

She breathed the question, "My son?"

The crowd surrounding us parted as if by magic and standing there was a boy of about four, holding the hand of an older girl. The boy looked just like a miniature version of my father, Two Eagles, except for his eyes. They were light green with flecks of brown. His head was shaved, as were all the children's heads. The girl led him toward us, holding his hand. He followed her, shy and hesitant.

When they stood in front of my mother, she fell to her knees and with outstretched hands murmured his secret name, "ToWawh Nu'KwiSus, my Strong Son?" He looked at her quizzically.

The girl introduced the child, "This is KeSaTo WeSKin, Light Eyes."

"My KeSaTo WeSKin, my lost boy is alive." My mother's tears of happiness were so plentiful they splashed as they hit the ground. The boy stood still for another moment and then tentatively reached for her hands. She pulled him close, and he folded himself into her body. He, too, was now home.

The PaTow'O'Mek survivors who had been working for Strangers at the time of the massacre now lived among the Portobacco, as were surviving members of the Nanzatico, another of the tribes that had suffered great loss of life and property in the summer of 1666. We were embraced and settled into the rhythm of life along the northern shore of the Potomac.

Eventually we explored the area of our former village. Settlers now farmed it and tobacco grew in orderly rows. On the northern edge of our land, the colonists had built a small fort with government buildings. Our life was not entirely peaceful. There was still tension among the Strangers and all the tribes as the Europeans kept arriving and demanding more land. We kept to ourselves as much as possible, trying to avoid confrontation.

My mother displayed a tranquility I had not seen or remembered in a long time. KeSaTo WeSKin was a gentle boy who listened eagerly to stories about his father. He already practiced hunting with a small bow and arrow. The Portobacco had loved and cared for him as one of their own.

The story was told that when the Stranger who had stolen him took him home, the man's wife said she thought the baby was possessed by the devil, she could tell by his eyes. It was his beautiful light eyes, the remnant of that long ago rape, that saved him and brought him to the safe keeping of the Portobacco. I had never stopped loving him either, and it was very natural to again be in the role of his big sister. After all, he was the first baby I had carried on my back before I gave birth to my own children.

In the Portobacco *Mesk YiHaKan*, I got my first tattoos. I never told my mother that my first blood had actually occurred on the *Mermaid* and so when I bled for the second time, the women celebrated my initiation into womanhood. My first tattoos were a flower and an eagle feather, an acknowledgment of my mother's strength and that of our friend Ah'SaWei. I had one on each shoulder so I could see them.

The first winter was very cold after living in Barbados for four years, but the fur pelts helped tremendously to retain heat. We continued to wear some of the cotton clothing we had become used to while living on the island. My mother told me about the linen rags the English women used for their bleeding time, and I was so happy to be a PaTow'O'Mek, and use moss instead that could then be returned to the earth.

Winter turned to spring, and I was to be married to a man who had survived the massacre because he had been away that night. I was happy about this and ready to transition into the life of a wife and mother. He was an expert hunter and had a reputation as a hard worker. He would be a good provider and partner. He brought gifts of dried corn and many seeds for planting to prove his value and worth. It had been decided that I would now live in his family dwelling, leaving my mother's home. We were in the process of moving my few belongings late one spring afternoon. We would start planting soon and wanted to marry before *CoHatTaYough*, the Time of Planting commenced.

Traders came through frequently. Our combined tribes still collected and ground antimony that was highly sought after. There were talented weavers of baskets, and some who could make the woven eel traps. Dogs lingered about the camp, but we were not actively trading them. A native trader from north of us casually mentioned during bartering that he had spoken with a PaTow'O'Mek survivor who lived in a place called New York. The word spread through our village, and we wondered who else had survived. We had so many questions for him. What was her name? Was she traveling with a young girl? What did she look like? Had she been in Barbados? He could not remember her name. No, she was not traveling with a child, she was alone. He said her face was severely scarred. He knew nothing about Barbados.

My mother and I did not speak of the news. It did not sound like our Ah'SaWei. She had beautiful clear skin. And she would not travel without MaNa. We could not bear the thought that something terrible might have happened to our precious Butterfly. So we did not speak of it. We were grateful that another PaTow'O'Mek woman had survived, and we held onto hope that Ah'SaWei and MaNa would find their way to us also.

The afternoon I was moving into my new husband's dwelling, we heard the sound of Big Dogs and through the opening in the palisade came the first two with their Lenape riders calling out, "*WinGaPo! WinGaPo!*"

Those of us outside, which were most of us in the late afternoon, looked with curiosity to see who was entering our village. Behind them came a third horse with a rider; it was hard to see if it was a man or a woman. Then I could see it was a woman, as her horse came between the two men, and she carefully dismounted. She began walking toward the gathered crowd. My mind could not comprehend what I saw at first, and then I screamed as loud as I could for my mother. She came running, fearing I was injured or worse.

When she saw Ah'SaWei standing there, she froze for the briefest of seconds before they ran to each other and collapsed into one another's arms. The words that could be heard through the tears of joy were, "*NihTe KihTe'*, my heart, your heart," over and over.

Over time, we heard the story of how Ah'SaWei and MaNa had escaped from Barbados. It could not be told all at once. The memories weighed too much, and it took time for the words to find air, such was Ah'SaWei's grief over losing MaNa and her husband, Levi. We learned of him and the great love they had shared. Ah'SaWei moved in with my mother and now it was my mother's turn to comfort her friend, comb her hair and lead her to the river to bathe as Ah'SaWei had done for NePa'WeXo so long ago. It was clear she was with child, and everyone in the tribe took her the choicest morsels of roasted eel and the heartiest portions of fish stew. As her belly grew, she began to look healthier, but the smallpox scars would mark her forever, telling the world she had survived a terrible disease. In the same way, the scars from the whippings and the branding of the letter T told stories of strength and survival of another kind.

Ah'SaWei gave birth to a healthy boy. His birth brought her great joy, but she was a muted version of her former self. She would never forget the losses she had endured. Her friendship with my mother and their shared knowledge of what they had survived helped to sustain her. She did not marry again.

* * *

I LOOK ACROSS THE FIRE AT THESE WOMEN and realize our tribe has survived because of their resilience. Their determination had kept me alive as well. Now here we are, the three of us, sitting among our people, each of us holding our babies. God willing, with the blessing of O'Ki'Us, Jesus and Yahweh providing, these children will grow up and thrive because of the strength of their ancestors and their will to live.

This is the story of the survival of the PaTow'O'Mek tribe of Virginia.

Glossary of terms
In Patawomeck, Algonquin and English

LANGUAGE NOTE:

The language of the Patawomeck tribe is being studied and re-learned with assistance from the early writings of William Strachey (1612) *The History of Travaile into Virginia Britannia* in which he recorded the language of the Powhatan tribes, the confederation of tribes that included the Patawomeck. It is an Algonquin dialect. The tribe currently uses *The Powhatan Dictionary* by Ian Custalow, compiled for his Powhatan Language Project. Many thanks and much gratitude are also due to Garry Cooper and David Moseley who have taught Patawomeck Conversational language classes to the children and adult tribe members for many years.

SEASONS:

CaTaPeuk - (Kaw-Taw-Pewk) Time of Fish Runs, spring, mid-March through April

CoHatTaYough - (Koh-Haw-Taw-Yoh) Time of Planting and Growing, May through July

NePiNough - (Neh-Pee-Noh) Time of Harvesting, August through September

TaQuiTock - (Taw-Kwee-Tohk) Time for Gathering Nuts and Hunting Deer, mid-October through mid-December

PoPaNaw - (Poh-Paw-Noh) Winter, mid-December through March

Words:

A'TeMos - (Aw-Teh-Mohs) Dog

BiCi - (Bee-Chee) Yes

DuNaPei - (Duh-Naw-Pay) Indigenous people living in Virginia, called "Indians" by Europeans.

GaKwa - (Gaw-Kwaw) Porcupine

HusKaNaw - (Hus-Ka-Naw) Rite of passage for boys, around age fourteen.

Keit WijhCats NaMeChe - (Cate-Weej-Kats Naw-Meh-Chee) dolphin, literal translation "Great fin fish"

KúHom - (Koo-Hoam) Your grandmother

ManGoi TeMos - (Mawn-Goi-Teh-Mohs) horse, literal translation "big dog"

ManGoi WeKoHis - (Mawn-Goi Wee-Koe-Heese) Great Hare, Creator of the Patawomeck tribe

MaTa - (Maw-Taw) No

MaCaNuTu WinKan - (Maw-Chaw-New-Too-Ween-Kawn) "We leave each other well," a parting blessing.

MaKaTaWai'Haw - (Maw-Kaw-Ta-Wah Haw) Blackhaw, a shrub the bark of which was boiled into tea and used to ease excessive menstrual bleeding and menstrual cramps. Also used to help maintain pregnancy.

Mesk YiHaKan - (Mesk Yee-Ha-Kan) Blood House, where the women isolated away from the men, during their monthly menstrual cycle.

Mu'Xom MeSeToNans - (Mew-Shom Me-Se-Toe-Nahns) Grandfather's Beard, a medicinal moss.

Nanzatico - (Nan-Za-Dee-Ko) One of the Powhatan nation tribes, also in Virginia.

Nek - (Neck) Mother

NihTe KihTe' - (Nee-Ta Kee-Ta) "My heart, your heart"; "I love you with all my heart."

Nir PaXeNa'An Nes - (Neer Paw-She-Naw-Awn-Nes) I will find you/I will flee to you.

Nu Hom - (New-Home) My grandmother

O'Ki'Us - (Oh-Kee-Us) One of the Gods of the Patawomeck and Powhatan tribes.

PaTow'O'Mek - (Paw-Tow-Oh-Mehk) Patawomeck, the Indigenous tribe living on the southern bank of the Potomac River, part of the Powhatan nation.

PipSisSeWa - (Pip-Sis-Uh-Wuh) Medicinal herb used by Indigenous people in Virginia and North Carolina.

Portobacco - (Poor-Te-Baak-Oh) One of the Powhatan nation tribes living on the northern bank of the Potomac River.

TasSanTasSas - (Tas-San-Tas-Sas) Strangers, unknown people to the Indigenous people, usually European.

TaMoKin - (Ta-Moe-Keen) Swim

TucKaHoe - (Tuh-Kuh-Hoh) A starchy tuber, dried, ground and used to make bread or thicken stew, still referred to as tuckahoe.

WinGaPo - (Ween-Gaw-Poh) Greetings to a fellow tribal member.

Locations:

MaNaHahTaAn - (Mah-Nah-Ha-Ta-Aan) Lenape for Manhattan in New York

Powhatan River - (Pau-Uh-Tan) Now called the James River in Virginia

Point Comfort - Now called Fort Monroe in Hampton, Virginia

ShaTeMuc - (Sha-Tay-Muck) Lenape name for what is now the Hudson River, New York

TseNaCoMoCo - (Se-Nah-Coe-Moe-Coe) Algonquin and Patawomeck word for Virginia

Other:

Sugar wine: early name for rum in Barbados

Barricado: wooden wall that separated the upper and lower decks, providing a barrier on the decks of the slave ships.

Calalu: stew made with okra, crab and coconut, introduced to Barbados and other Caribbean countries by the enslaved brought from Africa.

Pucoon: red dye; the plant from which the dye is made

Souse: soup made from snouts, feet and ears of pigs, boiled and marinated in a mixture of lime juice, peppers, onions, cucumbers and garlic, common in the Caribbean.

Further Reading

Bailey, Anne C. 2017. *The Weeping Time.* New York, New York: Cambridge University Press.

Custalow, Ian. 2012. *Powhatan Dictionary.* Stafford, Virginia.

Custalow, Dr. Linwood "Little Bear" and Daniel, Angela L. "Silver Star". 2007. *The True Story of Pocahontas.* Golden, Colorado: Fulcrum Publishing.

Gates, Henry Louis, Jr. 1988. General Editor. *Six Women's Slave Narratives.* New York, New York: Oxford University Press.

Gragg, Larry. 2009. *The Quaker Community on Barbados.* Columbia, Missouri: University of Missouri Press.

Haile, Edward Wright. 1998. *Jamestown Narratives.* Champlain, Virginia: Roundhouse.

Rediker, Marcus. 2007. *The Slave Ship: A Human History.* New York, New York: Penguin Books.

Rountree, Helen C. 2005. *Pocahontas Powhatan Opechancanough.* Charlottesville, Virginia: The University of Virginia Press.

Rountree, Helen C. 1989. *The Powhatan Indians of Virginia.* Norman, Oklahoma: University of Oklahoma Press.

Rountree, Helen C. 1993. Edited. *Powhatan Foreign Relations 1500-1722.*1993. Charlottesville, Virginia: The University of Virginia Press.

Rountree, Helen C. and Davidson, Thomas E. 1997. *Eastern Shore Indians of Virginia and Maryland.* Charlottesville, Virginia: The University of Virginia Press.

Rountree, Helen C. with Taukchiray, Wesley D. 2021. *Manteo's World*. Chapel Hill, North Carolina: The University of North Carolina Press.

Rountree, Helen C. and Turner, E. Randolph III. 2002. *Before and After Jamestown*. Gainesville, Florida: University Press of Florida.

Rountree, Helen C. and Clark, Wayne E. and Mountford, Kent. 2007. *John Smith's Chesapeake Voyages 1607-1609*. Charlottesville, Virginia: The University of Virginia Press.

Strachey, William. 1999. *A Dictionary of Powhatan*. Bristol, Pennsylvania: Evolution Publishing. (Reprinted from: Strachey, William. 1849. *The History of Travaile into Virginia Britannia*. London, England: Hakluyt Society. Which was a reprint of the 1624 edition.)

Stuart, Andrea. 2013. *Sugar in the Blood*. New York, New York: Vintage Books.

Zimmerman, Larry J. 2011. *The Sacred Wisdom of the American Indians*. New York, New York: Metro Books.

Enjoy more about
1666: A Novel

Meet the Author
Check out author appearances
Explore special features

ABOUT THE AUTHOR

A member of the Patawomeck Indian Tribe of Virginia, LORA CHILTON tells the story of her people and their unlikely survival due to the courage of three Patawomeck women. As a part of the process, she interviewed tribal elders, researched colonial documents and studied the Patawomeck language. Chilton graduated from Virginia Commonwealth University with a Bachelor of Science Degree in Nursing. She has worked as a Registered Nurse, a small business owner, an elected official, a non-profit executive and a writer. Memphis is her home. *1666: A Novel* is her second work of historical fiction.

Acknowledgements

I want to thank Sibylline Press for believing that this story should be told, especially Julia who immediately understood the characters and for her brilliant advice on what to cut and where to add. To Vicki, for her enthusiasm and kindness in moving the book (and me) through the publishing process. To Alicia, for her cover vision, which brought me to tears the first time I saw it. And to the rest of the Sibylline team, thank you.

I am forever grateful to the early readers who offered advice and encouragement: Barbara P., Jill S., Kim C., Sherri S., Barbara R., Ron C., Fredric K., Carol R., Kat K., Holly H., Carly K., Carol Lee R., Teresa B., Nancy A., Julie R. and Susan M.: thank you so very much.

To Julie J., Karen T., Jana T., Laurie S., Janis K., Jackie M. and Jamie M.: thank you for cheering along the way.

Many thanks to Teresa B. who traveled to Barbados to research with me when a COVID window opened. What an adventure!

To Sarah, Lisa and Mark: the greatest joy in my life has been to mother each of you. Your love and support, through thick and thin, means everything to me. And to the grands: Naomi and Fay, as voracious readers yourselves, your advice and confidence was just what I needed. Ezra, Lionel, Julian and Jack: I love you more than you will ever know.

Most importantly, to members of the Patawomeck tribe who have labored for years to save the stories, the language and the culture: KeNa, Thank you.

Book Club Questions
1666: A Novel by Lora Chilton

1. When Ah'SaWei (Golden Fawn) and Xo (Shining Moon) are taken as prisoners and sold to a slave-trader, they are assigned new names that are actually just numbers. Then, upon being sold again as slaves in Barbados, they are renamed with classic English names typical in the 1600s. The loss of their Indigenous names stripped them of one piece of their cultural identity, and they then had the status of property. Are there parallels in the modern immigrant experience where names are changed to facilitate easier assimilate in the United States? Are there parallels with the tradition of women taking their husbands surnames upon marriage? Is this always a choice?

2. The book describes the tradition of *Mesk YiHaKan*—seclusion of the women in the Blood House during menstruation that was a time of female fellowship and bonding. This practice has been observed in many cultures worldwide and is mentioned in the Bible in the Old Testament. Would observance of menstrual seclusion in modern times have any benefits? Or would it be detrimental socially for women?

3. The desire to return home fuels the women's will to live and likely gives them the fortitude to escape slavery in Barbados. Is there a primal urge to go home? Is home a place or a group of people?

4. Water imagery figures prominently in the story: the importance of the Potomac River to the life of the tribe, the vastness of the ocean as the women are transported to Barbados, the tropical water that surrounds the island. Other images are the warm rain and the sacred waters of the *mikvah* ritual cleansing bath. In what ways is water life-sustaining throughout the book?

Sibylline Press is proud to publish the brilliant work of women authors over 50. We are a woman-owned publishing company and, like our authors, represent women of a certain age.

Rottenkid: A Succulent Story of Survival
BY BRIGIT BINNS

Pub Date: 3/5/24
ISBN: 9781960573995
Memoir, Trade paper, $19, 320 pages

Prolific cookbook author Brigit Binns' coming-of-age memoir—co-starring her alcoholic actor father Edward Binns and glamorous but viciously smart narcissistic mother—reveals how simultaneous privilege and profound neglect led Brigit to seek comfort in the kitchen, eventually allowing her to find some sense of self-worth. A memoir sauteed in Hollywood stories, world travel, and always, the need to belong.

1666: A Novel
BY LORA CHILTON

Pub Date: 4/2/24
ISBN: 9781960573957
Fiction, Trade paper, $17, 224 pages

The survival story of the Patawomeck Tribe of Virginia has been remembered within the tribe for generations, but the massacre of Patawomeck men and the enslavement of women and children by land hungry colonists in 1666 has been mostly unknown outside of the tribe until now. Author Lora Chilton, a member of the tribe through the lineage of her father, has created this powerful fictional retelling of the survival of the tribe through the lives of three women.

I Never Do This: A Novel

BY ANESA MILLER

Pub Date: 4/16/24
ISBN: 9781960573988
Fiction, Trade paper, $17, 216 pages

This gothic novel presents the unforgettable voice of a young woman, LaDene Faye Howell, who finds herself in police custody recounting her story after her paroled cousin Bobbie Frank appears and engages her in a crime spree in the small town of Devola, Ohio.

The Goldie Standard: A Novel

BY SIMI MONHEIT

Pub Date: 5/7/24
ISBN: 9781960573971
Fiction, Trade paper, $19, 328 pages

Hilarious and surprising, this unapologetically Jewish story delivers a present-day take on a highly creative grandmother in an old folks' home trying to find her Ph.D granddaughter a husband who is a doctor—with a yarmulke, of course.

Bitterroot: A Novel

BY SUZY VITELLO

Pub Date: 5/21/24
ISBN: 9781960573964
Fiction, Trade paper, 18, 296 pages

A forensic artist already reeling from the surprise death of her husband must confront the MAGA politics, racism and violence raging in her small town in the Bitterroot Mountains of Idaho when her gay brother is shot and she becomes a target herself.

For more books from **Sibylline Press**, please visit our website at **sibyllinepress.com**

Printed in the USA
CPSIA information can be obtained
at www.ICGtesting.com
JSHW021359250324
59871JS00004B/124

9 781960 573957